ANGEL IN PERIL

ARGONAUT
THE INUA HUMPBACK

BOOK TWO

Suzie,
Best wishes.
Hope you enjoy the book.

Cliff Scovel
&
Argonaut

ANGEL IN PERIL

ARGONAUT
THE INUA HUMPBACK

BOOK TWO

BY

CLIFFORD L. GIONET

Argonaut Humpback Productions

ILLUSTRATIONS BY SUSAN B. SPAIN

PHOTOGRAPHIC EDITING OF ILLUSTRATIONS BY KIM DAVIDSON

VANCOUVER ISLAND MAP PRODUCED WITH MICROSOFT PAINT

PROUDCTION ASSISTANCE BY JESS ELLIOTT

Manufactured in the United States of America

ACKNOWLEDGEMENTS

People who live and work in Telegraph Cove have provided me with inspiration for this book. Captain Jim, Mary, Jackie, staff of Spirit Bear Lodge, wonderful volunteers at the Marine Education Research Society (MERS), and dedicated staff at Orca Lab brought my ideas to life. All these individuals and groups were the inspiration for *Angel in Peril* and the predecessor title, *Argonaut the Inua Humpback*.

Without the magnificent humpbacks, orcas, dolphins, Spirit Bears, eagles, and other creatures of the marine sanctuary this story would not have been possible.

Jess Elliott has become my mentor, friend, and production assistant. Without her, neither this book or the first in the Argonaut series would have been published.

The illustrations by Susan Spain are valued additions to the book. Her gift of the illustrations to help raise money for the Marine Education Research Society is deeply appreciated.

Photographic assistance with the illustrations, to get them in proper format, was provided by the very talented photographer and photoshop expert Kim Davidson.

My wife, Peggy, has been my partner and greatest supporter for over thirty-five years. Without her, my life would have no meaning.

This book, like the first in this series, is dedicated to my late son Jason for whom Argonaut was named by wonderful friends at the Marine Education Research Society. One person writes the words, but it takes many people for the words to become available to readers.

Any errors are the fault of the author.

MARINE EDUCATION RESEARCH SOCIETY

The Argonaut series of fiction novels is written in hopes of raising funds for the non profit group Marine Education Research Society (MERS). This small, dedicated, hardworking, understaffed, and underfunded group of volunteers is trying to save earth from the destructive forces of climate change and pollution. They live and work surrounded by the magnificent creatures of the Vancouver straits in western Canada.

MERS staff are inspiring people who seem to have unlimited energy. They measure their successes in small gains. The successes are vitally important. You can research MERS, Orca Lab, and Spirit Bear Lodge on the web. The scenery of the Vancouver straits area is beyond description. The majesty, beauty, and magnificent animals have left an indelible mark on my life.

100% of the royalties from publication of Argonaut the Inua series, is being donated to MERS. f you'd like to make a contribution, please send a check to:

MARINE EDUCATION RESEARCH SOCIETY
Box 1347
Port McNeill, British Columbia
CANADA V0N 2R0

TABLE OF CONTENTS

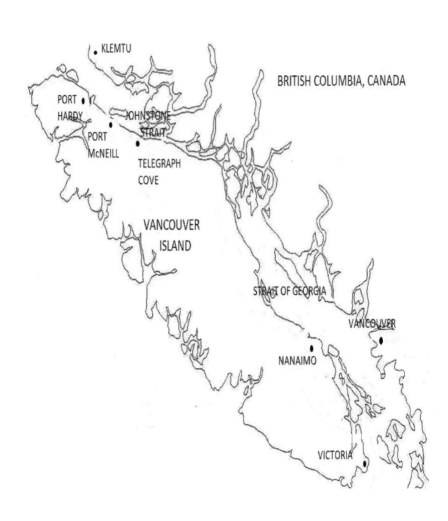

PROLOGUE

In the first book of the series, we met Argonaut the Inua Humpback. A large A was seared on his tail when he was struck by lightning on the day of his birth, Argonaut lives most of the year with his pod in the straits near Vancouver Island, British Columbia.

His best friend is Jason Belliveau. Jason and Argonaut learned to communicate using the Wet PC underwater computer. As Argonaut's Inua talents grew they were able to communicate telepathically.

Angel is Argonaut's mate. She is easily identified by the perfectly shaped angel wings on her tail. They have a son named Raven. In book one, Raven gets trapped in a large fishing net and almost drowns. There is a confrontation with orcas trying to attack humpback calves. Argonaut leads a negotiation between great white sharks and a group of orcas and humpbacks to keep great whites from entering the marine sanctuary.

A group of young Kitasoo students form a group called Project HOPE. The movement begun by the young First Nation people captures the attention of millions of people around the world as they attempt to save the planet from the effects of climate change and pollution.

History, science, and adventure are all part of the stories told in *Argonaut the Inua Humpback.*

In *Angel in Peril,* we meet many new characters. Argonaut continues his involvement in rescues and exciting events.

While the first two books in the Argonaut series are meant primarily for young adults, readers of all ages seem to enjoy the stories.

SAVING GREAT WHITE SHARKS

Sitka's pod was returning to Vancouver Island from their winter home in warm waters of the Hawaiian Islands.   As the pod approached the north Vancouver Island marine sanctuary, Argonaut felt danger to great white sharks that swam in the Pacific Ocean near western Vancouver Island.

Argonaut used his Inua telepathic skill to ask his son Raven and another male humpback, Guardian, to swim with him towards the distressed great whites. Argonaut wanted to save a great white in danger. Argonaut told Sitka, matriarch of his pod, to continue swimming with her pod to their sanctuary. The three adult males would rejoin them, as soon as possible.

Raven asked his father what was happening.

Argonaut said, "There is a young great white trapped in a fishing net. It is going to be killed for its fins. The disfigured carcass will be thrown back into the ocean, if

1

we do not help. Swim as fast as you can. We have to save the great white before it is killed."

Raven asked what they were going to do.

Argonaut told his son, "First, I will contact the great whites using my Inua powers. I will tell them we are on our way to help. I will explain my plan to you and Guardian as we swim. Hurry."

Last year, in a confrontation with five great whites at the entrance to the marine sanctuary, Argonaut had negotiated a truce between the two species. He promised great white sharks a peaceful co-existence if the great whites stayed in ocean waters and did not invade the marine sanctuary. In return, if these great white sharks needed assistance, humpbacks would help. Argonaut was honoring his promise.

Three humpbacks swam south from the northern entrance to the straits of Vancouver Island. Argonaut reached out to sharks using his thoughts.

One shark answered Argonaut.

He said, "My son is trapped in a fishing net. Land creatures will cut off his fins and kill him. We need your help."

Argonaut said, "Of course, we will help. We have a plan. We will be at your side as quickly as possible."

Argonaut explained his plan to Raven and Guardian. Both agreed to do their part.

Argonaut sent a message to the sharks. The Inua explained what needed to be done. As soon as the three humpbacks arrived, they would coordinate a simultaneous breach on three sides of the fishing boat. A large great white would breach on the fourth side of the boat where a fishing net holding a young great white was being winched aboard ship.

As three whales and one great white breached, other sharks would use their sharp teeth to destroy the net to release the trapped shark. Sharks agreed with Argonaut's plan. They waited for the three humpbacks to arrive.

The boat hunting and killing sharks was a fifty-foot steel-hulled trawler from Japan. The boat was in international territory. It was not in violation of current international law to hunt and kill sharks. The Inua and his friends had promised to help great whites. Argonaut was a creature of integrity. He would sacrifice his life, if necessary, to help save his shark friends.

The three humpback whales arrived. They finalized

their plan, in coordination with the sharks. It was time to execute a rescue. Three whales and one shark breached next to the boat. Fishermen on board were stunned and scared. This had never happened to these fishermen before. Multiple simultaneous breaches distracted the fishermen. Two great whites attacked the net. Using their sharp teeth, they were able to cut through the tough net. They released the trapped shark.

Great whites thanked the three humpbacks for their help. Argonaut reminded them of his promise. He told the sharks his pod would always be friends with great white sharks.

As the sharks swam into deeper waters, Argonaut used his Inua power to speak to the fisherman.

Argonaut said, "No longer will you hunt sharks and kill them for their fins. Humpback whales and great white sharks of these waters are friends. We will fight you. If you continue to harm sharks we will breach until your boat sinks. You will become food for the same sharks you often kill. Do you understand?"

The fishermen did not know who was speaking to them. They had seen what whales and sharks working together could do. Terrified, the fisherman promised to stop hunting sharks.

Argonaut warned the fishermen to leave and not return. Argonaut told the fishermen to tell other shark killers of the fury and wrath demonstrated by humpbacks and sharks. If shark slaughter did not cease, humans would become the hunted and not the hunters. Terrified fishermen promised to heed Argonaut's warnings. They would share the story of friendship between British Columbia humpback whales and great white sharks.

Argonaut had a faint sense of another Japanese trawler, also outside of Canadian waters, trying to catch and kill sharks for their fins. Fisherman were killing many different species of sharks. Argonaut felt his anger swell. He used his Inua powers to reach out to Wild Bill Mendenhall, Commander of the western Canadian Coast Guard.

"Hello, my friend. Do you know who this is?" Argonaut asked the commander.

"Of course, I know who you are. It is not every day that I get mind messages from an Inua humpback. How are you and your pod?" asked the commander.

"We're fine. May I ask you a favor?" Argonaut inquired.

"It would be my honor to help. What can I do?" said

5

Mendenhall.

"There are fishing boats near Vancouver Island catching sharks, cutting off fins, and throwing the bodies into the ocean. My friends and I just scared off one boat, but another fishing vessel is nearby. Is there anything you can do to discourage these fishermen from killing sharks for their fins?" Argonaut asked.

"If the boat is in international waters, we cannot legally intercept them. Captain DeFord is nearby with his ship Canadian Coast Guard Ship (CCGS) Risley. He and his crew are probably bored with routine patrol duties. They may be able to make a close pass by the trawler. The Risley might instill a little fear in the fishing boat crew. We may accidentally get a little too close. We might create a substantial wake with our propellers. It is possible that while engaging in live fire target practice, a few fifty-caliber machine gun rounds, including tracers, could possibly come very close to the bow of the trawler. We would certainly mention to the trawler captain that this area is not safe for shark hunters since we often use the area for live round firing practice. We will explain that it would be in their best interest to sail away. The CCGS Risley's wake, machine gun fire, and verbal message may give the fishermen pause," Mendenhall said.

"That is a great idea, commander. These men are killing sharks, not for food but for profit based on some bizarre legend that shark fins have mystical powers. This horrible practice needs to stop," Argonaut said.

"I agree with you. I will contact Captain DeFord. I will suggest he have a conversation with these fishermen. We will try to discourage their habit of slaughtering sharks," said Commander Mendenhall.

"Thank you, commander," the Inua said.

Good to his word, Mendenhall called DeFord on his cellphone. He did not use his official Coast Guard radio. This was an off-the-books suggestion that Mendenhall did not want recorded.

"Jim, this is Bill Mendenhall. I just learned that trawlers are operating near Canadian waters killing sharks for their fins. I find the act reprehensible. I wonder if your ship might make a very close pass by this trawler. The CCGS Risley could create a substantial wake to get their attention. See if you can dissuade them from killing sharks," said the commander.

"Boss, I hate seeing these animals killed. My crew spotted them on radar fifteen minutes ago. We will make unofficial contact within next twenty minutes. A few rounds of our fifty-caliber machine gun across their bow might be persuasive.   I will call you back in thirty minutes," DeFord said.

The CCGS Risley cut across the bow of the trawler missing the ship by a few feet. Captain DeFord used his loudspeaker to instruct the trawler to stop all engines. The captain was angry. He instructed the fishermen to cease and desist killing of sharks.

The trawler crew knew they were in international waters. They told DeFord they were doing nothing illegal. Now DeFord was truly upset. He instructed his forward gunner to fire a few hundred practice shots across the bow of the stopped trawler. The gunner was happy to get in some practice. Hundreds of fifty-caliber machine gun rounds, including some tracers, came within feet of the trawler. DeFord had a nickname among his crew. He was called "Captain Doom". When he was mad, it was something to fear. He was very mad at the trawler crew.

The fishermen understood they had no choice but to comply with DeFord's suggestion to leave. The trawler left sailing west, at top speed.

Captain DeFord used his cellphone to call Wild Bill Mendenhall.

He told his superior officer, "Mission accomplished. We fired a few practice rounds. The target understood our intentions. Trawler last seen steaming away from our island. My guess, we will not see them again."

"Great job, Jim. We will keep this between us and your crew. Make sure they keep their lips sealed," said Mendenhall.

"Understood sir. CCGS Risley over and out," said Captain DeFord.

Argonaut had followed the operation using his still growing Inua powers. He reached out to Commander Mendenhall and thanked him.

Argonaut, Raven, and Guardian entered the sanctuary right behind Sitka's pod. Argonaut touched his son and Guardian using his thoughts. He told them how happy he was to be home. They both agreed.

It was early spring. The skies were clear, the water cool and comfortable. Bait fish seemed abundant. There is no place like home.

THE INUA STORY

After several days rest, Sitka asked Argonaut to listen to more tales passed down from earlier generations of memory keepers. If Argonaut was to be next memory keeper of their pod, he had much to learn.

Sitka spoke to Argonaut, "Legends of Inua have been told by many creatures of land, sea, and air. I have heard that far away, in the direction where the sun appears each day, there are people who believed in Inua since time began. In their world, all creatures have a spirit. Inua can be either good or bad. Inua of these people have great respect for all animals of earth, water, and sky. These land creatures, from where the sun comes out of the water and over the trees each day, think the spirit of every creature must be treated with reverence. To them, all creatures have an inner being. Animals deserve honor, even in death. When they kill a seal or bear, they pray for the animal's spirit. Respect for the spirit of all life is part of Inua traditions of these far away people."

Sitka continued, "Another people, from where great white sharks first came, also believe in Inua. People and animals can both be Inua. To these people, Inua is a thing that makes a person or animal good and kind.

There are other Inua stories of creatures with great powers. You are a powerful Inua. We have seen you speak to many creatures. You can control minds of land creatures, orcas, and great white sharks. You can foresee future events. You may be the most powerful Inua of all time," Sitka said.

"Did memory keepers tell stories of Inua like me?" asked Argonaut.

"I have heard stories of creatures with powers like yours. Legends tell of a great battle between good and bad Inua living in the sky. Bad Inua were banished from the sky and doomed to live in darkness deep underground. Good Inua stayed in the sky above land and water. Good Inua were said to help all creatures.

Memory keepers talk about Inua that are bigger than we are. These giant Inua live in faraway places. I have heard stories about these Inua. One legend tells of an

11

Inua who lived near our winter home. A giant demon tried to kill a good Inua. The Inua had a son who had powers like yours. The good Inua saved his mother from the evil monster. This is the story of Hina and Maui.

In a land near where the sun goes at night, there is another legend of a powerful Inua. This Inua ruled over wind, water, and storms. This Inua was called Shenlong," said Sitka.

"I feel my powers grow with each passing day. Will I always be a good Inua?" Argonaut asked.

"I have known you since the day of your birth. You are kind, brave, and a seeker of peace. You have never shown anger or unkindness. I am certain you will always be a good Inua. You are destined for greatness my young friend," Sitka said.

Argonaut asked Sitka if he would always be able to do the right thing.

Sitka thought about her answer. "I know you will always do your very best without fear. You saved our pod from orcas, then made peace with them. You protected us from great white sharks, then made peace with them. I have never heard of a more powerful and kind Inua," said Sitka.

Argonaut felt impending danger to Angel. No matter how hard he tried, he could not see future events clearly enough to be certain he could protect Angel. He saw Angel in a dark place. In his visions, Angel was taken from their sanctuary. He felt helpless. He was afraid. Even his great Inua powers might not be enough to save his mate.

Argonaut and Sitka returned to their pod and swam in the beautiful and safe marine sanctuary waters.

A cloudless sky of bright blue failed to lift Argonaut's spirit. He knew trouble was at hand.

JASON AND ARGONAUT MEET AGAIN

Returning to the marine sanctuary was a relief to Sitka's pod. The whales were exhausted after migrating from Hawaii. The adults had not eaten in more than five months. The pod soon settled into a normal routine of eating and sleeping in the safe waters of their home.

Argonaut's Inua powers were rapidly increasing in scope. He could reach out, using his telepathic power, to many creatures over longer distances. Argonaut was getting more glimpses of future events.

Argonaut called out to his human friend Jason Belliveau. He soon heard his friend's thoughts welcoming the pod back to Vancouver Island waters. Argonaut asked Jason when they could meet. Jason suggested dawn the following day at the entrance to Telegraph Cove.

As the sun was rising above towering aspen and spruce trees of western Canada, Jason and Argonaut met at a bay not far from Telegraph Cove.

Jason asked, "How was your winter in Hawaii?"

Argonaut responded, "We are all safe and have three new young calves in our pod. We are happy to be back."

Argonaut told Jason of his encounter with a shark fishing boat. He told his friend how he, Raven, and Guardian helped save a captured great white. He also explained how Commander Mendenhall and Captain DeFord helped drive off another trawler before more sharks were killed.

Jason asked, "Does it seem remarkable to you that humpbacks and sharks can co-exist in peace?"

Argonaut said, "In stories told by humpback memory keepers, there are many legends. One story tells of a time, many ages ago, when all creatures of the land, sky and sea lived in peace. One day everything changed. Humpbacks, orcas, and sharks were no longer friends."

"What happened?" Jason asked.

"Legend says that land creatures were first to start killing. Fighting and violence spread to all creatures of earth, sky, and sea. It was as if something horrible had

15

happened. Land creatures no longer wanted to share earth with animals," Argonaut said.

Jason told Argonaut the biblical story of Adam and Eve. The first two humans disobeyed God's order. They ate the forbidden fruit. They were expelled from the Garden of Eden. After fleeing the Garden of Eden, humans had to hunt and kill for food.

"Perhaps that was the beginning of conflict between land creatures. It may also be the start of violence against animals," Argonaut said.

"This story may just be a figment of someone's imagination. No one knows if the story is just a legend and not fact. We don't know that the Garden of Eden was an actual place," Jason said.

Argonaut said, "Your land creature story of the Garden of Eden sounds similar to humpback legend of a sudden end of peace among sea animals."

"How are Angel and Raven?" Jason asked.

"Raven is almost as big as I am. He has proven to be a great source of joy and pride to me. He helped defeat the shark fishermen and save a great white. He was not afraid. Angel is my best friend. We are happy together," said Argonaut.

Argonaut asked Jason about widespread illness he sensed in many land creatures.

Jason explained, Novel Coronavirus (COVID-19) was infecting millions of people worldwide. The pandemic caused hundreds of thousands of deaths.

Argonaut learned from his matriarch, Sitka, legends of other great sicknesses affecting land creatures. Long ago, there was a disease called the plague or black death. Another worldwide pandemic called Spanish Flu had killed millions of land creatures.

Argonaut's Inua senses told him, soon the Coronavirus would almost end for this year. Argonaut knew the disease would return in winter to kill many more land creatures. The Inua told his friend that a medicine would be discovered within two winters to help save land creatures. Argonaut knew there was nothing he could do except be as helpful to his human friends as possible.

Argonaut explained to Jason that he had a deep sense of foreboding about future events in the marine sanctuary.

"What do you think is going to happen?" asked Jason.

"I see two large ships from a faraway place. Angel will be taken from me," Argonaut told Jason.

"How can a ship take Angel when she can swim so fast and go so deep?" Jason asked.

Argonaut replied, "We are being watched by flying objects high above us. I feel a strong presence of evil and danger. I am afraid I will not be able to save Angel from darkness I sense all around her."

Jason asked Argonaut if he was certain of future events.

"As my Inua skills strengthen, future events become clearer. I am sure Angel will be taken from me. I am not certain I will be able to save her," said Argonaut.

Jason tried to calm Argonaut by explaining Coast Guard ships and helicopters would detect any invaders that entered the marine sanctuary.

Argonaut said, "The Coast Guard may be able to help. It will take all my Inua powers, you and your friends, and many other sea creatures to save my mate."

Jason promised to help any way he could.

Argonaut and Jason said their goodbyes. Argonaut rejoined his pod.

As Jason was traveling home aboard his boat Sadie Princess, he thought about what Argonaut had said. As a drone operator himself, Jason understood that drone technology was advancing rapidly. Was it possible that drones were observing his interactions with whales of Sitka's pod? Could Angel actually be kidnapped from the sanctuary?

Jason called Commander "Wild Bill" Mendenhall, who knew of Argonaut's Inua talent. Jason told Mendenhall of Argonaut's worry of Angel being kidnapped. Jason explained in detail exactly what Argonaut saw happening in the future.

Commander Mendenhall said, "There are no foreign ships in our waters that are not registered as cargo transport vessels. There are foreign ships outside our territorial waters from many different countries. We have no jurisdiction in international waters. It would be a violation of law to fly aircraft over Canadian land or water without Canadian governmental approval. If someone takes a humpback from our waters, we will respond with all resources at our disposal."

Jason said, "We have both witnessed Argonaut's ability. I worry he may be right about drones being involved in Angel's kidnapping. If some foreign government or corporation has discovered Argonaut's talents then he and others of his pod may be in danger."

"Why would anyone want to kidnap Angel when Argonaut is Inua?" asked Commander Mendenhall

"I do not know. Perhaps kidnappers think all whales in Sitka's pod have Inua powers. What can we do to help our whale friends?" Jason said.

"It is a difficult time for all of us in the Coast Guard. Coronavirus has affected almost twenty percent of my seamen. Many of our ships are idle due to a shortage of sailors. I will ask the Provincial Governor of British Columbia to request the United States use their satellite tracking capability to monitor ship activity in the north Vancouver Island area. I will ask that we be alerted if any ships enter our territory without permission," the Commander said.

"Thank you, Bill. I will tell Argonaut that you are doing all you can to help," Jason replied.

What Commander Mendenhall did not know was that the Provincial Governor of British Columbia, the Premier of Canada, and more than half of the legislators of Canada were ill with COVID-19 virus.

Current tensions between the United States and Canada over trade barriers and tariffs hampered cooperation between the two countries.

The United States refused to help patrol Canadian territory for foreign pirates. The commander's request for satellite observation of the Vancouver straits went unanswered.

The thought of losing Angel to foreign kidnappers was disturbing to Jason. He reached out to Matt Hawk and his father, Captain Jim Hawk. While on a video conference call, he told father and son that a whale who was special (they knew he meant Argonaut) had a problem. The special whale and his family needed their help. Jason explained this special whale had a deep foreboding of his mate being kidnapped. They avoided using Argonaut's name in case their calls were being monitored.

Both Captain Jim and Matt knew enough about Argonaut's powers to believe Jason's story.

"What can we do?" Matt asked.

Jason said, "You both know many boaters around Vancouver Island. Will you ask them to be on the lookout for any large foreign vessels in Canadian waters? If anyone learns of such a ship, they can notify me. I'll ask Commander Mendenhall to send help, if he can. Also, please ask people who live near the Pacific Coast to look for large ships from other countries that are near Canadian territory."

Both Captain Jim and Matt promised to do all they could to help prevent Angel's kidnapping. As members of the Canadian Coast Guard Auxiliary, they had close contacts with many boaters in Vancouver waters. Certainly, someone would spot foreign ships entering their marine sanctuary.

Jason reached out to Argonaut and told him what Commander Mendenhall had said. He relayed the offer of assistance by Matt and Captain Jim.

"How soon do you think foreign pirates will kidnap Angel?" Jason asked.

Argonaut replied, "Before the sun disappears five times."

This meant Jason had five days or less to help Angel.

Matt suggested mounting video cameras on both sides of the north harbor of Johnstone Strait. They would monitor cameras for ship activity. These cameras are motion activated. Any ship entering or leaving Johnstone Strait would activate cameras.

"Great idea," said Jason.

"We can have live feeds sent wirelessly to our phones. If we detect any activity, we can alert the Coast Guard and ask for their help," Matt said.

"We can also have the feed sent to Orca Lab since there is someone on duty there all day, every day," Jason said.

Jason called his friend Diane at Orca Lab. She and her co-workers agreed to help monitor camera activity.

Jason spoke to Argonaut with his thoughts. The Inua whale joined him at the entrance to Telegraph Cove where Jason was waiting aboard his boat Sadie Princess.

Jason explained his plan to Argonaut. The Inua whale was still unsettled by his vision of future events.

"It is a good plan but not it may not be good enough. My senses tell me that Angel will be taken in spite of our efforts," said Argonaut.

Argonaut told Jason that he would stay close to Angel. He would try to protect his mate to the best of his ability. What neither Jason nor Argonaut knew was that the foreign threat to Angel would come by air, not by sea.

Jason and Matt installed action activated cameras on trees surrounding the northern entrance to Johnstone Strait. Argonaut swam next to his mate and worried.

Argonaut explained his fears to Angel, Raven, and the rest of the pod. Sitka asked what the pod should do. Argonaut suggested the pod stay at the southern end of their sanctuary. If any ships entered the strait from the north, Matt and Jason would have time to call the Coast Guard for help.

The southern entrance to the straits was near the cities of Victoria and Vancouver. It was unlikely a ship could enter from the south undetected. There was more security around the large cities of Vancouver and Victoria.

DANGER FROM ABOVE

Thirty miles west of Vancouver Island, in international waters, two large container ships were motoring north from Seattle, Washington in the United States. Both ships flew the flag of Panama but were not Panamanian craft. These ships had originally sailed from North Korea.

Many ships flying the flag of the small Central American country of Panama are not owned by Panamanians but by foreigners. Most countries have stricter laws about maritime safety, than does Panama.

Panama has an open registry for vessels. You can register your ship online for a modest fee. Using this process, you can avoid foreign taxes and use cheaper labor.

The tiny country of Panama has more ships registered to its flag than the United States and China combined.

Two large ships approaching Vancouver Island were manned by Panamanian pirates hired by an undercover agent of the North Korean government. The pirate ships were moving towards Canadian waters to kidnap one of the whales spotted by drones during encounters between Jason and the Sitka pod.

People behind the attempted kidnap were not certain of Inua whale talents. They had seen enough, using spy drones, to want one of these special whales.

The plot to steal one of Sitka's whales had been in the planning for two years.

On a night with no moon, two drones would be deployed to where humpback whales were living.

Each drone carried eight concussion grenades that would be used to stun the whales. Once the whales were rendered immobile, two large Russian Mi-26 helicopters with stealth technology, for blocking visibility by radar, would deploy from one of the ships. Helicopter pilots would pick one whale. Gunners would shoot the designated with a paralytic drug rendering the whale immobile. The drugged whale would be unable to swim, dive, or flee.

Once a whale was tranquilized, divers from the helicopters would enter the water. They would attach two large slings underneath the whale floating at the surface. Once the whale was secured, divers would return to the helicopters. Both slings would be fastened to the underside of each helicopter. Aircraft would fly in unison to lift the drugged whale. The rotary aircraft would fly back to their ship carrying the kidnapped humpback. The captured whale would be lowered into a holding tank especially designed to secure a mature humpback. The tank is large enough to accommodate a stolen humpback whale. The tank was filled with sea water circulating in its interior. The whale kidnapping had been practiced many times using a large floating metal container filled with ballast and shaped like a whale, in waters off the coast of North Korea.

Pilots and divers were equipped with night vision goggles. In spite of almost complete darkness, the pirates could see clearly.

Russian Mi-26 helicopters are each capable of carrying fifty-thousand pounds of cargo. Mature humpbacks weigh in excess of sixty-thousand pounds. It would take two helicopters to transport a captured humpback to a ship.

The motion activated cameras Matt and Jason had deployed would be no help. Satellite images were not available because of reduced surveillance staffing issues related to the Coronavirus. Trade war tensions between the United States and Canada insured that help from Washington would not be available.

As night fell, Argonaut sensed impending danger. He urged his pod to gather together in the deepest waters of the Strait of Georgia. Argonaut thought he could protect his pod, if all whales stayed close to each other.

Spy drones approached the pod from the west. Drones could not be heard over sounds made by waves and wind. North Korean drones, developed and built in China, were equipped with full stealth technology. They were fast and virtually invisible.

Sixteen concussion grenades were dropped from two drones. At that instant, Argonaut told the pod to dive deep and fast. He knew there was danger coming from the sky.

All humpbacks, except Angel, made the quickest and deepest dives they could. Angel was gape feeding, was distracted, and was slower than other whales to heed Argonaut's warning.

Grenades detonated. Even Inua Argonaut was stunned, his senses were dulled. Whales lost their ability to swim. Some floated on the surface while others started sinking to the bottom of the strait.

One Russian helicopter carried an expert marksman who shot Angel with a dart containing a strong drug. North Korean scientists had determined the proper dosage of Xylazine Hydrochloride to use on a mature humpback. If the correct dosage is administered, this is a safe sedative and potent muscle relaxer. The paralytic substance rendered Angel immobile.

Angel was unable to swim. Divers were immediately in water attaching giant carrying slings under Angel.

Angel was unconscious as she was lifted by two giant Russian built helicopters.

Other whales slowly recovered their senses. All whales were able to return to the surface and breathe.

The last thing Angel remembered was Argonaut telling all whales to dive quickly, as deep as they could. Angel tried to dive but she was paralyzed by the drug shot into her by a large dart.

As Angel woke, she sensed she was in a large container. Her echo locating senses told her the holding space was barely bigger than her body. There was no room to turn. She could rise a few feet to breathe stale air but she had no way to escape. The water was unclean. There was no food.

Using her thoughts, she tried to reach Argonaut. Angel did not sense her mate near her. She used whale sounds to call Raven. Her son did not respond. Angel could hear familiar rumblings, like boats, passing in waters near Vancouver Island. Angel felt certain she must be on a large boat. She was alone and afraid.

Angel was being held captive in a container ship bound for a foreign country far away from her home and family.

Argonaut and his pod were stunned by grenades but not captured. After recovering from the grenade attack, Argonaut could not find Angel. He tried calling her using whales sounds. He used the full force of his mature Inua powers, but she was not in the sanctuary.

Argonaut asked if any of his whale family had seen or heard what had happened to Angel. No one remembered anything except the loud noise of grenades and being stunned. Whales had been unable to swim until effects of the concussion grenades wore off.

Stun grenades used by North Korean directed pirates were a larger version of ones used by police to immobilize criminal suspects. These types of weapons are also used by military fighters against opposition in battle.

Argonaut used his Inua powers to repeatedly call out to Angel. There was no response. Argonaut had seen fragments of the future but not enough to protect his mate. The great Inua was helpless, frightened, and uncertain of what to do.

Argonaut called out to orcas and pacific white-sided dolphins who lived in the straits near Vancouver Island. He talked to these marine creatures. He asked if any of them had witnessed Angel's kidnapping.

The father of the orca Argonaut had saved last year, after being cut by a propeller, said two giant machines had lifted Angel skyward. Two mechanical birds (helicopters) flew in the direction where the sun disappears at day's end.

A dolphin said he had seen two large ships off the coast of Vancouver Island. Two large metal birds had dropped a whale into a hole of a ship.

Argonaut thanked his friends. He reached out to Jason. Argonaut explained to Jason what had happened to Angel.

"Jason, Angel was taken by two large flying machines to a ship on the ocean side of our island. I can't sense her with my Inua powers. I need your help," said Argonaut.

"How long ago was she taken?" Jason asked.

"It was dark, there was no moon. It was not long ago," answered Argonaut.

"I will call Commander Mendenhall and see what he can do. Coronavirus illness is still making many land creatures sick. He and the Coast Guard will help, if possible," Jason explained.

"Please hurry," Argonaut pleaded with his friend.

Jason called the Coast Guard station in Victoria and found Commander Mendenhall there.

"Commander, Angel, mate of Argonaut, has been kidnapped from the Strait of Georgia by two helicopters. They flew west probably less than two hours ago. Kidnappers used what must have been stun grenades to immobilize the pod. Angel was taken. What can we do?" Jason asked.

"I know the general in command of the Seattle station of the United States Air Force Command. I will ask him to scramble fighters. They will try to locate the ships. Even if we can find the ships, we have no proof Angel was taken from Canadian waters," said Commander Mendenhall.

"Yes, we do. I put tracking tags on all members of Sitka's pod. I can verify by logged tracking history on my computer where she is at any time. The tags are accurate within a radius of one mile. Even if the signal is jammed, I can prove where and when she was stolen. I tagged all Sitka's whales because Argonaut was afraid for Angel," said Jason.

Argonaut was listening to the two men talk. He reached out to both with his Inua powers.

Argonaut said, "If you can locate the ships, I have a plan to stop them."

The Coast Guard officer said, "Under Rule 98 of the International Maritime Convention, a ship is obligated to help any other ship that is disabled and possibly in harm's way. If the pirate ships could be stopped due to a mechanical failure, we would be required to tow them back to safe harbor in Vancouver. Once the pirate ships were in our waters, we could arrest the pirates and free Angel."

"How can you possibly stop a ship large enough to carry a full-grown humpback?" Jason asked his Inua friend.

"Find the ships. My marine animal friends will stop them," Argonaut said.

Commander Mendenhall called General Rene Lee-Pack, commanding officer in charge of the United States Air Force Command in Seattle.

"Rene, it is Bill Mendenhall," said the Canadian Coast Guard commander.

"Wild Bill, it is great to hear from you. How are things in Vancouver?" General Lee-Pack asked.

"We have a problem. We need air support. One of our whales was kidnapped by pirates using helicopters. At least two pirate vessels are somewhere off the western coast of Vancouver Island. Do you have any planes you can scramble and help us find our missing whale?" asked Commander Mendenhall.

"I have a fighter squadron lifting off right now for a training mission. They can be in the area within ten minutes. Do you know what we are looking for?" asked General Lee-Pack.

My guess, there are at least two large container ships vectoring west from our island. One may have two big helicopters on deck. The other ship must have our whale in a hold. The theft occurred within the last two hours," said Commander Mendenhall.

Seattle Air Command was flying a squadron of F-35 Lightning II aircraft. These are the most modern fighters in the US Air Force. The F-35 II combines advanced stealth technology with tremendous speed and fully fused sensor information. If any planes could find Angel, these US fighter planes could.

"My birds have heat sensing technology. We should easily be able to get a reading on a humpback even in a hold. What do you want us to do when we find the ships? We can't intercept. That would be a violation of international law and an act of war," said the general.

"We have a special group of friends who are going to assist the ships become disabled. We will be required, under international law, to tow the ships back to Vancouver," the commander said.

"How in the world will these two ships become disabled simultaneously? You certainly can't attack them or you will provoke an international incident," said General Lee-Pack.

I have a confidential source that believes there is a lot of floating debris in that area of the ocean. My source told me it is possible, in fact likely, both ships may become entangled in floating debris. Once the pirate vessels are dead in the water, they will require our assistance," said the commander.

General Lee-Pack laughed and said, "You Canadians are a crafty bunch. I will contact my flight squadron. The flight leader will radio you once the pirates are located. I hope you get your whale back. Good sailing, Bill," said the general.

"Thank you, Rene. Next time you are in Vancouver, dinner is on me," the commander said.

General Lee-Pack contacted the squadron commander. He gave instructions on locating the pirates. The squadron leader was Colonel Angela Choate. Colonel Choate had graduated first in her class at the US Air Force Academy. She was a veteran of many combat and search and rescue missions. She had named her airplane "Relentless". Like her, Relentless was the best of the best.

Argonaut reached out to his friends; the great white sharks, orcas, and pacific white-side dolphins who lived west of Vancouver Island. The Inua explained his plan.

"I need help from all of you to save my mate. Send your fastest swimmers towards where the sun goes at end of day. In that direction is the boat that holds Angel. I sense a second ship, near the first, that carries two mechanical birds that lifted Angel into the sky. Once the ships are located, we will stop them. Working together we can save my mate," Argonaut said.

"Do you know how to stop a ship?" asked the largest great white shark.

"We will work together as a team. I have seen ships broken because the thing that makes the boat go was wrapped in a net. Raven was once trapped in a large fishing net. If a net could trap Raven, it can stop a ship. I know this plan will work, if we hurry. The thing that cut the young orca last year is what we must stop from turning. If we can find a large net, chain, long piece of metal, cable, or anything to wrap around the spinning blades at the back of the ships, we can stop the pirates. If we can stop these ships, my land creature friends will save Angel. Will you help me, please?" pleaded Argonaut.

Sharks, orcas, and dolphins started swimming west as fast as they could. They spread out. The animals soon heard engines powering large ships. Argonaut could not keep up with these faster animals. He could, however, read their thoughts. Humpbacks are much slower swimmers.

Within ten minutes of takeoff, US Air Force fighters located both ships. The US squadron called location coordinates to Commander Mendenhall. The commander notified Captain DeFord on board CCGS Risley to proceed to help a ship in distress at the coordinates provided by US Air Force planes. The commander also notified Jason of exact coordinates of Angel's location. Jason verified, using the tracking device implanted in Angel's tail, US fighter planes had located the right ships. Jason told Argonaut where to direct orcas, sharks, and dolphins.

Jason verified to Commander Mendenhall marine animals had also located both pirate ships. Animals, under Argonaut's direction, were working on a plan to disable both vessels.

Captain DeFord had not heard any distress calls. He followed orders and proceeded at maximum speed to coordinates provided by his commander.

Orcas, dolphins, and great whites were swimming towards the North Korean pirate ships, heading west from Vancouver Island.

Commander Mendenhall received a radio call from US Air Force pilots who were doing reconnaissance in rescuing Angel.

"Commander Mendenhall, this is Colonel Angela Choate of the 5th Air Force wing from Seattle. Do you, copy?"

"Colonel Choate, I read you five by five. What can you tell me about these pirate ships?"

"There are two heavy cargo ships about fifteen kilometers west of Vancouver Island. Heading away from the island at about ten kilometers per hour. One ship has tarps over what appear to be two large rotary aircraft. A second ship is giving off a large heat reading from a hold midship. I think the second ship has your lost whale," the US officer said.

"My whale was not lost. Pirates stole her from my waters. This is personal with me. We must get her home. Colonel Choate, we have an intercept ship on course to coordinates you provided. We should make contact within ten minutes," Commander Wild Bill said.

"We have enough fuel to fly a holding pattern for another three hours, if you need us," said the Air Force pilot.

"I have information that leads me to believe the second ship, with our whale, is going to fall on hard times. Both ships may require rescue under International law. Thanks for your help," said Commander Mendenhall.

The air force pilot replied, "You're welcome, Commander. Always glad to help our northern neighbors. We will stand by in case there are any problems that require our eyes in the sky or our firepower. Over and out."

As the CCGS Risley was nearing intercept with both pirate vessels, marine mammals and sharks were also rapidly approaching. The animals sent their thoughts to Argonaut. They asked what they should do.

Argonaut explained they needed to find a cable, chain, or netting, and disable both ships. The largest orca told Argonaut that his pod saw a large net floating nearby. They would take netting and dive under the boat holding Angel. They would try disabling the ship.

As orcas dragged netting, sharks and dolphins prepared to wrap the large net around the ship's propeller. Argonaut told orcas to let dolphins take netting under the boat since they were faster swimmers. Great whites held ends of heavy netting until the propeller started wrapping netting around the ship's drive shaft.

As netting wound tighter around the drive shaft and propeller, the ship's engines worked harder until they overheated. The ship came to a dead stop.

Just as the ship started to drift without power, Captain DeFord and his crew appeared on scene aboard CCGS Risley.

Argonaut could not swim fast enough to join his friends so he had to listen to events as they unfolded. His heart was racing. He tried to reach out to Angel but he still could not sense her.

Argonaut called out to orcas, dolphins, and great whites. The Inua told them they must also stop the second ship. People who took Angel must all be brought back to Canada to face justice for harm done to Angel. Argonaut was furious. His mate had been taken from his side. He had never felt so powerless. It took all his resolve not to stop the pirates' beating hearts. He knew, if he acted in anger, he would betray the Inua powers that have been so helpful to his pod.

Two great whites dove to the ocean floor. They found an abandoned anchor chain lost in a storm. Sharks lifted the chain, with help of dolphins and orcas. The animals wrapped the chain around the drive shaft of the second boat. Soon the second pirate ship, with two helicopters on board, was drifting without power.

Argonaut reached out with his Inua senses and told Commander Mendenhall that both ships had been stopped. Pirates and their ships could be brought back to Canada and Angel freed, if she were still alive.

Commander Wild Bill radioed instructions to Captain DeFord.

Mendenhall told Argonaut that he was certain Angel was still alive because US fighter planes had read a large heat source on board one of the pirate vessels. If Angel were not alive, there would be no heat readings. This news was a great relief to Argonaut. He wanted to believe that his mate was safe, but he had to see her for himself.

Jason was also certain that the heat readings were from Angel. Her electronic tag was emitting a signal from the same coordinates as the two pirate ships.

"Captain DeFord, my intelligence says both pirate ships are disabled. Under maritime law you are bound to help these vessels. Only safe way to protect ships and crews is to tow them back to Vancouver for repairs," said Commander Mendenhall.

"Understood Commander, but my boat can only tow one pirate ship. What do I do with the second ship?" Captain DeFord asked.

"Jim, in about ten minutes a US Navy frigate returning to Seattle from a tour in Alaska will be at your location to offer assistance. They should be on your radar. They are heading in your direction," said the Commander.

"Do we need to worry about any interference from foreign powers while a rescue operation is underway?" the captain asked his commanding officer.

"As it happens, I have a friend in the US Air Force, Colonel Angela Choate, who is going to have her flight squadron do training exercises right over your position until you are in Vancouver harbor. There is also a US Navy submarine standing by two miles off your stern to offer assistance, if needed," said the commander.

"Aye, aye sir. As soon as the US Navy boat arrives, we will start back to Vancouver. We will have both ships back in Vancouver harbor within two hours," said Captain DeFord.

PROJECT HOPE CONTINUES TO GROW

The small group of young Kitasoo students, who started Project HOPE (Help Our Planet Exist), were working tirelessly to expand membership in the group. The young First Nation tribe members were doing everything in their power to save our world from self-destruction. These young Kitasoo understood that world leaders and governments would only respond to pressure from a large group of concerned citizens. HOPE needed to recruit as many members as possible,

Jill White Feather, Susan Standing Bear, Jim Wildhorse, Joan Redclaw, Mary Raven, and Charles Windsong are original members of Project HOPE. Last year, after a student trip aboard Orcella 2, the group decided to do their best to stop rapid destruction of earth's environment due to climate change and pollution.

Over fifteen-hundred Project HOPE chapters were operating in forty-two countries. More than three-million members now belong to Project HOPE chapters. Progress was being made. Change was happening but danger from climate change was increasing. Antarctic temperatures recently exceeded one hundred degrees Fahrenheit for the first time in recorded history

The world's largest carbon polluters are oil companies including Shell, Chevron, and Saudi Aramco. Refineries are spewing pollution at record levels. HOPE members are exerting increasing pressure on refiners and drillers to reduce their role in climate damage. Countries are raising the miles-per-gallon requirements for new vehicles being produced. Banks are reducing or eliminating funding for oil and gas exploration in ecologically sensitive areas, like Alaska and Amazon basin. Germany just committed to a plan that will end the country's coal and nuclear power plant energy production within ten years.

The United Nations, by request of its security council, scheduled a world conference in Paris for October 2021. The meeting was to frame new international legislation to reduce climate damage and global warming. Even non-democratic governments understood the world cannot continue to get warmer without our entire planet facing disaster.

The United States of America, which had previously withdrawn from the Paris Climate Accords, was willing to participate in finding solutions. Hopefully, a newly elected administration and congress would help lead the United States towards helping find solutions to these worldwide dangers.

Plastic bottle manufacturers, like Coca Cola, Pepsi, and Nestle, are now heavily taxed in most countries to enhance recycling. There were economic and legislative initiatives passed in most countries to encourage a switch to using glass or other bottling techniques, not as destructive as plastic containers. A new plant-based bottle is being developed by a Dutch company. The bottle will disintegrate within two years of production. Project HOPE was providing world-wide exposure for ecologically sound companies on their website.

Governmental taxing authorities are collecting carbon taxes from heavy polluters. Government leaders are providing new economic incentives for polluters to reduce their carbon footprint.

Major corporate entities, including Wall Street financial concerns, agricultural companies, auto manufacturers, and industrial producers, are adopting Project HOPE goals designed to reduce pollution. Every major company in the world is graded by HOPE for its climate change impact. Major offenders are being ostracized by consumers. International boycott of major brands, not in compliance with HOPE goals, is having a positive effect on corporate behavior.

The Doomsday clock has slowed its progress. There was much more to be done. There was less time to accomplish HOPE's objectives. There was still a slight chance the world could be saved.

All major religions on earth were now actively supporting Project HOPE. Catholics, Jews, Muslims, Hindus, Protestants, Buddhists, and virtually every other faith were banding together to help change earth's environment. A healthy life is part of everyone's right. Religious leaders understood the need for immediate actions. Congregations worldwide mobilized to fight pollution and climate change.

What began in a small First Nation village on the island of Klemtu, by six high school students, was now one of the world's most powerful forces for saving our planet.

One of Project HOPE's major objectives was to get young people active in politics. During the Vietnam War, students protested and registered to vote in ever increasing numbers. As was true during the 1960s, youthful voters now want to elect candidates who understand the need for radical, cultural, and behavioral changes. Leaders were needed who understood the need for action, if life on our planet is to survive.

For the first time, technology was being used as a leading weapon to effect change. Facebook, Instagram, YouTube, Twitter, and other social media platforms were being used by HOPE chapters. The message was clear. Potential disaster could be averted only if significant change started immediately.

Media outlets were asked by influential sponsors to support the goals of millions of members of Project HOPE. Apple, Microsoft, Amazon, Alphabet, Alibaba, and many other large business concerns now understood, if climate change was not reversed there would be no consumers to buy goods and services.

No one knew if there was enough time left to fix climate problems. For the first time, there was a concerted, organized plan worldwide attempting to save life on earth.

The six original members of Project HOPE from the Kitasoo tribe were so busy with HOPE work there was no time for them to attend school.

The Kitasoo Xai'xais tribe elders hired two tutors to take up residence in Klemtu. The tutors' job was to help

Project HOPE leaders stay current in their studies and graduate with their classmates in May 2021.

LeeAnne Gionet and Sarah Clark were retired teachers from Calgary who accepted tutor positions on Klemtu. Both tutors wanted to experience the wonders of the Queen Charlotte Islands. They looked forward to working with six remarkable students who were trying to save our world.

Sarah planned to teach Kitasoo students sign language so they could sign their messages in the many video broadcasts sponsored by HOPE.

Klemtu had vacant cottages, perfect for the tutors to occupy during their stay on Klemtu.

ANGEL STILL NOT SAFE

As Captain DeFord was preparing to tow the Panamanian registered pirate ship holding Angel, the littoral combat ship USS Independence (LCS 2) reached the rescue operation site. A littoral ship is one that can operate in shallow waters close to shore.

The Independence was commanded by Captain John S. (Steve) Waters. The US Navy Captain called DeFord on the radio and said, "Ahoy, Risley, the USS Independence is at your service."

"Glad to see you captain. I want you to tie off the second ship. Please, prepare the ship for towing to Vancouver drydock for repairs. Apparently, its drive shaft got damaged. The ship is disabled," said Captain DeFord.

"It has been a long time, Jim. How have you been?" asked the US Captain.

"All is well, Steve," said Captain DeFord.

Captain Waters said, "I think the last time we met was during a training exercise in the Strait of Georgia in 2018."

"That's right. We are so busy with our commands that time seems to slip by. Do you think you'll have time to stop in Vancouver after we drop off the pirates?" asked DeFord.

"My sailors are anxious to get home. We have been in Alaska for six months. Maybe next time we are in the area, we can have dinner and swap stories," Captain Waters said.

"Steve, the ship we are towing has a kidnapped whale in a hold amidships. The one you are towing has two helicopters that were used in the kidnapping. The copters are stored under tarps on mid-deck," said DeFord.

"We have four of your Air Force jets flying cover for us. There are no reported ships of unknown origin within two-hundred miles. One of your submarines is following us about ten miles astern," said DeFord.

As two military ships towed the pirate vessels towards Vancouver, Argonaut heard the officers' conversations in his thoughts. He knew Angel was on her way home. He could not reach her with his mind. He did not know for certain if she were dead or alive. He wanted to believe the pilot who had recorded heat from Angel on her sensors. Until he heard her thoughts and saw her alive, he was anxious.

Argonaut asked Sitka if he and Raven could travel to Vancouver to meet the ship with Angel on board.

Sitka said, "Go, be with your mate. We are safe here since you made peace with the orcas."

Argonaut called to his son, Raven, to join him. The father and son humpbacks started swimming towards Vancouver harbor.

As they were swimming south, Argonaut reached out to Commander Mendenhall. He asked Mendenhall to have CCGS Risley rescue Angel from the tank as soon as possible. She needed to be in fresh waters of the Strait of Georgia.

Commander Mendenhall passed orders to Captain DeFord who responded in the affirmative.

When both the USS Independence and CCGS Risley reached Vancouver, they were met by a squad of Royal Canadian Mounted Police (RCMP), officers from Canadian Immigration Service, and several members of the Department of Canadian Oceans and Fishery Department.

The two pirate ships were docked. Crews were taken into custody by law enforcement officers for interrogation.

Captain DeFord called Captain Waters on the radio and said, "Safe trip home Steve. Thank your crew for us. We are kind of serious about our humpback whales in Canada."

"Jim, let me know how all of this turns out. Stay well and safe travels. USS Independence over and out," said Captain Waters.

The USS Independence left Vancouver harbor and headed for her home port in San Diego, California. Colonel Choate called on her radio to verify that all was well before she and her squadron returned to Seattle.

"Colonel Choate, it made us all feel much better knowing your F-35 birds were flying cover. Thank your base commander for us. CCGS Risley, over and out," radioed Captain DeFord.

"Our pleasure Captain. We have never been involved in a whale rescue before. US Air Force 5th Flight wing, over and out." The jets climbed at full throttle. The F- 35s roared back towards Seattle.

The US Navy submarine that had been following the rescue efforts glided silently into the depths. The sub went back to normal patrol duties off the west coast of the United States.

As requested, Captain DeFord had dock workers use two large cranes to carefully lift Angel from the dark hold and slowly lower her into the Strait of Georgia.

Argonaut and Raven had reached Vancouver harbor as Angel was being placed into the water. The Inua told Angel, using his thoughts, to be calm. He told his mate not to move until land creatures had her safely in water.

Once Angel was free of the rigging, Argonaut and Raven swam to her. The family spoke in whale sounds and songs. The instinct of whales, even Inua, is to sing at times of great emotion.

Argonaut told Angel the story of her kidnap and rescue. Angel was exhausted and hungry. She wanted to swim back to their pod.

Argonaut said, "I am with you now. I will never lose you again. My Inua powers are increasing. You and our son are my life. I would give my life for either of you. I feel I failed you when you were taken. I will be more vigilant and careful in the future."

"Inua mate, you have made peace with orcas and sharks. You have made friends with land creatures. Your friends saved me. Don't be so hard on yourself. All is well. We are back together in our home waters. Soon we will be with our pod," Angel said.

Argonaut knew this was not the end of dangers that he, Angel, Raven, and Jason would face. For now, he would keep his thoughts to himself. He wanted to enjoy having his family by his side.

HOME AGAIN

Argonaut, Angel, and Raven swam slowly towards their pod in a bay near Orca Lab.

They slept and ate. Angel regained her strength. Humans do not understand animals can dream. Angel would have dreams of her captivity in the dark and dank hold for many months.

As they were swimming north, Argonaut reached out, using his Inua power, to thank orcas, dolphins, and great whites involved in saving Angel.

The eldest orca female replied, "You made peace with orcas and saved a young orca cut by a ship. We were glad to help our humpback friends."

The largest great white said, "You, your son, and friend helped save one of my family. It is right that we do the same for you and your family. Be safe my friend."

Jason called out to Argonaut and asked if all was well. Argonaut replied the pod was all together again. Commander Mendenhall and his friends had saved Angel.

"I am forever in debt to Commander Bill," said Argonaut.

Jason and Argonaut agreed to meet the next morning at the same beach where the young orca had been saved. They had much to discuss.

At sunrise, Jason arrived on his boat, Sadie Princess.

Argonaut was waiting. Jason put on his dive gear and joined Argonaut.

"How are you, friend?" asked Jason.

"I am at peace now that Angel is back with us," Argonaut replied.

"Why do you think bad land creatures stole Angel?" asked Argonaut.

"I have thought a lot about that. I think we were seen talking by someone using spy drones. Our conversations may have been witnessed when we first used the Wet PC to talk to each other. The water is so clear that we may have been photographed underwater using the computer and flash cards when we began our conversations. The people who paid the pirates said they wanted to capture a whale who could talk to humans," said Jason.

"Do you think the danger is over?" asked Argonaut.

"I don't know. I have asked Commander Mendenhall to request more satellite fly overs of our home. We constantly need to look for foreign ships. There are cameras in place at the north end of Johnstone Strait. Coast Guard boats will patrol entrances to our straits more frequently. Matt, Captain Jim and I have asked all boaters we know to keep an eye out for strangers," Jason said.

"I will be more vigilant and alert. I should have sensed danger before we were hurt by blasts that made us unable to move and Angel taken by evil men," Argonaut told his friend.

"Argonaut, there is an old human saying that says, we learn more from our mistakes than our successes. You are a powerful creature. I think your mate will be safer now," Jason said.

COVID-19 VIRUS STRIKES THE KITASOO

S pirit Bear Lodge had cancelled all visits when the Canadian government ordered a quarantine and self-isolation due to COVID-19. Unfortunately, one visitor on the last trip, that did reach the Lodge, was infected with the virus. Several members of the tribe were stricken with the Novel Coronavirus disease.

There are no hospitals or doctors on Klemtu. There are no ventilators, test kits, or other modern medical tools.

Kitasoo tribe members followed all recommendations of Canadian governmental medical directives. The two tutors, now living on Klemtu, had been trained in first aid. They had practiced their medical skills during volunteer trips to help poverty-stricken residents in several Central American countries. LeeAnne and Sarah assumed control of the medical situation until additional help could arrive. Isolation protocols were enforced.

The infection vector was spreading the illness quickly among the tribe. Help was desperately needed. Chief White Feather called his old friend, Captain Hawk, and asked if professional medical help could be sent to Klemtu.

Captain Hawk called Commander Mendenhall.

"Bill, is there any way we can fly a doctor, ventilator, masks, and gloves to Klemtu?" asked Captain Jim.

The commander called the governor of British Columbia. He agreed to send the requested supplies and a doctor to Port Hardy the next day. Klemtu had become a world-renowned location because of Project HOPE. The world was watching with great interest what was happening to the six famous Project HOPE directors and their families on Klemtu

Lieutenant Commander Pierstorff and her co-pilot Captain Bruce Brient met a supply plane in Port Hardy. Supplies were transferred to the Coast Guard helicopter. Dr. Wendy Harris joined the flight crew. Pilots and Dr. Harris made the quick trip to Klemtu.

Dr. Harris and helicopter flight crew unloaded equipment and supplies at the entrance to the tribe's Big House. Dr. Harris was updated on the condition of all sick

Kitasoo. She was pleased isolation protocols were in place.

The helicopter departed. Dr. Harris dressed in a mask, protective face gear, gloves, and gown. She started treatment for ill First Nation tribe members. Fortunately, neither LeeAnne nor Sarah was infected by the virus. They had used homemade masks and fishing gloves as protection before modern medical supplies arrived.

Jason Belliveau had previously been accepted as a full member of the Kitasoo tribe. MERS had donated one-million dollars to the tribe from the sale of an Inuit serpentine sculpture of a humpback. The sculpture had been given to Jason by Raven. Jason had helped saved Raven's life after he had been trapped in a large fishing net. MERS and Jason were deeply involved with Kitasoo life on Klemtu.

As soon as word of the virus infecting Klemtu was broadcast around the world, many HOPE chapters offered to send supplies. Jason acted as courier and transported supplies from Port Hardy to Klemtu on his boat, Sadie Princess. Matt Hawk accompanied Jason on many trips to Klemtu.

Lieutenant Commander Pierstorff and Captain Brient flew food and other supplies to First Nation tribes in locations north and east of Vancouver Island. Before the pandemic struck, British Columbia ferries would bring supplies to the isolated islands. By government order, all ferries were forced to stop traveling, due to risk of spreading the virus.

The Big House on Klemtu was converted into a hospital ward where infected tribe members were quarantined. Only Dr. Harris and two tutors acting as medics were allowed into the makeshift hospital. All three wore full protective clothing. They worked tirelessly to save tribe members sickened by the virus.

No visitors were allowed to visit Klemtu while isolation and quarantine were required.

Klemtu's sickest patient was Chief White Horse. Dr. Harris appealed to Project HOPE chapters for a ventilator to save the chief's life. A ventilator was offered by the government of Japan and flown to Vancouver. Lieutenant Commander Pierstorff and Captain Brient picked up the breathing device in their Coast Guard helicopter and flew it to Klemtu.

Dr. Harris and the tutors serving as emergency medics met the helicopter. The ventilator was rushed to the Big House.

Chief White Horse was put on the breathing machine and within a few days started to breathe easier. White Feather was a strong and sturdy man. He was, however, seventy-two years old. He was in the high-risk group. Severe illness and possible death from the virus were more common among the elderly.

As the Shaman and tribe members prayed, Dr. Harris and her medical assistants worked without a break for six straight days. Finally, the chief's fever broke. He could now breathe without aid of the ventilator.

All tribe members infected by the virus were improving. After two weeks of isolation, life was returning to normal in the village of Klemtu.

The ventilator was flown back to Vancouver by the two Coast Guard pilots. The breathing-assist machine was put to use in a Vancouver hospital serving many sick people infected with the disease.

Students of Klemtu fell behind in their studies because of virus conditions. Tutors, LeeAnne and Sarah, installed Khan Academy educational software on each laptop, smart phone, tablet, and desktop computer on Klemtu.

Once the new software was installed, the tutors could see how each student was progressing in their studies.

Tutors could devote time to students who were struggling in any particular subject. Khan Academy software was free. Both tutors had experience using Khan software from their church sponsored trips to Central America, on education missions.

Khan Academy lessons are available for every subject and grade level.

Soon the Kitasoo students, using Khan software and help from their tutors, were progressing through their schoolwork at an accelerated rate.

THE MYSTERY OF INUIT IN BRITISH COLUMBIA

As the COVID-19 pandemic subsided, Jason and Argonaut returned to their routines. The friends often met in various bays and harbors. Jason took pictures of underwater wonders in the marine sanctuary while Argonaut and his pod swam nearby.

Jason asked Argonaut, "Are you ready to tell me where you and Raven found the serpentine stone whale sculpture?"

"Raven and I will take you to a place of ancient humans, where the sculpture was found," said Argonaut.

"Follow us in your boat. It is not far," Argonaut told his friend.

They traveled about five miles to the site of a large rock slide. Argonaut told Jason to anchor his boat and put on his black diving suit and breathing equipment. Jason put on his scuba gear. He joined the whales in the clear, cold water.

"Where are we going?" asked Jason.

"This place was once flat like many islands in our home waters. One day, many seasons ago, the earth shook. All the land creatures who lived in this spot were covered by rocks that were thrown into the air from the ocean. They all died," said Argonaut.

"How do you know about this?" asked Jason.

"Sitka told me the story as part of my learning memories of our pod. Memory keepers of each generation have passed the story along to the next," Argonaut explained.

"Where did you and Raven find the Inuit stone sculpture?" Jason asked.

"There is a hidden entrance to an underwater cave that only a few sea animals have seen. Follow us. We'll take you to the forgotten land of ancient creatures," Argonaut said.

Jason, Argonaut, and Raven dove about one-hundred feet below the surface of calm bay water. Argonaut and Raven together pushed a large boulder to one side. The opening to a vast underwater cavern was exposed.

The three friends crossed into a cavern. This space was like the ancient whale burial site Argonaut and Raven had previously visited on their quest. There was light and fresh air.

The cavern opened to a flat area. The cavern encompassed about one-hundred-thousand square feet. The cavern was filled with ancient shields, spears, canoes, skeletons, and Inuit art. This was where the Inuit had come. This is where they had died.

Jason marveled at such an incredible diversity of artifacts. The entire history of western Canada was wrong. The Inuit had come to the Vancouver area. They had not flourished. They had died under tons of rocks probably caused by violent upheavals from an earthquake or long forgotten volcano.

Jason was excited. He wanted to take some samples of Inuit culture, for study by Vancouver museum experts.

Argonaut read his mind and warned, "If you disturb this ancient site, it will violate a sacred burial ground. If this place is known to land creatures it will be swarmed by boats filled with people looking for valuable art. Please Jason, leave this place to the spirits of those who lived and died here. Your people would want their burial sites to be honored and left undisturbed."

"You are right. This place is holy and must not be discovered by treasure hunters. It has been left intact exactly as we see it, for thousands of years. I will not violate such hallowed ground," Jason said.

Argonaut explained to his son what he and Jason had decided. Raven nodded his head in agreement.

Three swimmers left the cavern. Argonaut and Raven pushed the large boulder into place, blocking the cave's opening.

Jason felt like the first modern man who opened the Great Pyramids in Egypt. However, unlike the theft and destruction of Egyptian wonders and artifacts, there would be no grave robbers visiting this hidden Inuit cave in western Canada.

Jason followed Argonaut and his son back to Telegraph Cove.

"Thank you my Inua friend. That was one of the most exciting underwater experiences of my life. I will keep the burial site a secret. Inuit ancients will not be disturbed," Jason told Argonaut.

As the Inua and his son left to rejoin their pod, Jason reflected on all the incredible events, journeys, and adventures he shared with Argonaut.

SAILBOAT ADRIFT

Now that the Coronavirus pandemic had subsided, British Columbia ferries, tour boats, and recreational craft were again motoring in both Johnstone Strait and the Strait of Georgia.

One evening, with a new moon and almost total darkness, a fifty-foot sailboat named Fish Tales was anchored near Hanson Island.

Fish Tales is a Hunter 50AC sailboat built by Hunter Marine of Alachua, Florida. The hull of the boat is a fiberglass-balsa combination above the water line and a solid fiberglass construction below. Fish Tales was built in 2019. It was transported by truck to from Florida to San Francisco, California. This was the maiden voyage for Fish Tales. There were six people on board ship when it anchored near Vancouver Island.

Crew were inexperienced sailors. This was the biggest boat any of this crew had ever sailed. Winds were favorable for a northward trip from Vancouver. It had been a long day. Everyone went to sleep early that eventful evening.

A storm blew in from the Pacific. Waves, rain, and lightning grew in severity. The crew thought their boat was well protected, at anchor near the island.

The person who had the midnight to three in the morning watch fell asleep. He did not notice Fish Tales break its anchor line. The inexperienced crew had failed to leave running lights on. The ill-fated boat was virtually invisible in the darkness. Fish Tales was floating into the main channel of Johnstone Strait.

Strong tide and currents started to move Fish Tales into harm's way just as a British Columbia ferry boat, Quadara Queen II, approached Hanson Island. The Quadara Queen II ferry was returning to its home station of Port McNeill just north of Telegraph Cove. The ferry was built in 1969 in Vancouver. It was more than three times the size of Fish Tales.

Captain Coral Denton, aboard Quadra Queen II, was a veteran of twenty-five years piloting craft in straits of Vancouver. She had a perfect safety record. Just as the larger ship rounded a bend, Fish Tales suddenly drifted into the ferry's path.

Captain Denton had no time to sound an alarm or stop the large ferry. Quadra Queen II struck the stern of Fish Tales.

As the large ship reversed engines and turned on all spotlights, the smaller sailboat was sinking rapidly. Because of the sound construction of the smaller craft, everyone on board was able to safely evacuate wearing their life vests. Fish Tales sank into depths of the strait.

Captain Denton called the Canadian Coast Guard. She reported an accident had just occurred. She provided the location's coordinates so rescue operations could begin. Coast Guard officials said it would be at least thirty-minutes before rescue craft would arrive at the crash site. There was a skeleton crew on Quadra Queen II. There were not enough sailors to attempt a recovery of people in the water. Crew aboard the ferry tried throwing lines and additional floatation devices to swimming survivors. High winds, waves, and almost zero visibility made it hard to reach survivors with rescue lines.

These waters are home to transient orcas who are meat eaters. Orcas heard the crash. They were drawn to the cries of survivors. Black and white torpedo-like orcas swam toward flailing swimmers. Water was cold. Wind was blowing. It was hard for swimmers to see land.

Just as the first orca was about to attack a victim, Argonaut appeared. He placed himself between the orcas and struggling land creatures.

"Stop, my orca friends. These land creatures mean you no harm. They need our help," said Argonaut.

The eldest female orca said "We made peace with humpback whales not with land creatures. They are food to us. We want to eat as we please. As long as we do not attack humpbacks, we have not broken our promise."

"Land creatures are much more powerful than orcas or humpbacks. If they decide to hunt orcas your kind will cease to exist. This sanctuary is a place where no one will harm you, unless you attack land creatures. I know this to be true because once my kind was almost hunted to extinction by land creatures," Argonaut said.

One young male orca decided to disobey Argonaut. He started to swim towards a crash victim with his jaws wide open.

Argonaut used the full force of his Inua powers on the young orca. He reached deep into the mind of the attacking orca. Argonaut forced the orca's mind to go blank. The young orca was stopped before he reached any swimming survivors. Suddenly this young orca understood, Inua had power to stop his mind. Argonaut the Inua could even stop his heart, if he did not obey.

"We are friends in this sanctuary. I know you are meat eaters, but there are seals here for you. You can eat salmon, if you choose. You must never, for your own safety, attack land creatures. We worked together to keep great whites from our home. Let's work together to save these humans. If we show them kindness and mercy, they may one day help us," Argonaut said.

Argonaut released his control over the young aggressive male orca who swam slowly back to his pod with downcast eyes.

The matriarch of the orcas asked how they could help the land creatures survive.

"They are not like us. This water is too cold for them and they will drown if we do not get them to land soon. Find a rope from the wreck. Drag the rope behind you. I will tell land creatures to grab onto a trailing line. You can pull them to shore," Argonaut explained.

Three orcas each grabbed a drifting rope. Argonaut used his powers to tell the land creatures to grasp a line and hold on. Orcas would save them by pulling them to a nearby island beach.

As rescue by orcas was started, BC Ferry Captain Denton was watching the events with her binoculars. Even with ferry search lights, it was hard to see exactly what was happening. It looked as if three orcas were dragging ropes being held by passengers from the wreck of Fish Tales. Captain Denton had been sailing the inland passage to Alaska for more than thirty years. She had never seen anything like this rescue of humans by killer whales.

Within fifteen minutes, all survivors were safely ashore at West Cracroft Island. They were wet, cold, but they were safe. Argonaut used his Inua power to erase memory of the rescue from the minds of Fish Tales survivors, Captain Denton, and crew of Quadra Queen II. There would be no report by these people of seeing orcas tow people to land from these people. There were other witnesses Argonaut did not see.

CCGS Risley, first vessel on scene, had been on patrol not far from the accident. Captain DeFord deployed two rigid zodiacs to West Cracroft Island. Risley crew helped survivors transport from beach to the rescue ship.

Captain DeFord called Captain Denton aboard Quadra Queen II. Captain DeFord said all survivors were accounted for and safely aboard CCGS Risley. The ferry captain said she was turning her ship around, heading to Vancouver for an inspection and needed repairs before continuing to Port McNeill. There was no way to know if her ship had been damaged by striking Fish Tales.

The sailboat sank in about eight-hundred feet of water. The wreck was no danger to boat traffic. Insurance company representatives would send a recovery team to attempt a salvage of the sailboat.

The young orca who had defied Argonaut and attempted to attack swimmers apologized to the Inua. "You've been a good friend to my species, and I should have listened. I'll be more respectful in the future of Inua wishes."

"It is natural to seek out food. It is our instinct to want what we need to survive. No forgiveness is required. I was a young whale once. I sometimes acted against wishes of my matriarch. Be well, my young friend," Argonaut said.

"Thank you, great Inua. I hope we can always be friends," said the young orca.

It had been a long night for orcas and Inua. All animals returned to their pods for rest.

JASON THE BLOOD-STOPPER

In stories told in northern Maine, eastern Canada, and in some southern areas of the United States, there are tales of faith healers called Blood-Stoppers. In lumber camps of New Brunswick, in the late nineteenth and early twentieth centuries, Blood-Stoppers were held in high regard.

Accidents with saws, falling trees, and axes often left lumberjacks with horrific wounds and profuse bleeding. Legends say the eldest son of a Blood-Stopper has the power of his forefathers.

Jason was the eldest son of Jean-Luc Belliveau, who was the eldest son of Joseph Belliveau. Joseph had been a renowned Blood-Stopper. Jean-Luc reportedly saved two people from bleeding to death in New Brunswick. If this legend was true, perhaps Jason had the same healing

power as his father and grandfather.

In early August 2021, a strong earthquake hit northern Vancouver Island. Epi-center of the tremor was located approximately twenty-two miles due west of Telegraph Cove. All buildings in Telegraph Cove shook. The kayak center collapsed. Four people were trapped in wreckage.

Jason was visiting the Hawk family when the earthquake struck. After tremors stopped Matt, Captain Jim, and Jason all ran into Telegraph Cove to survey damage. They would try to help victims trapped in wreckage and debris.

First building they approached, after leaving the Hawk's home, was the kayak center. The three friends heard cries for help from people trapped inside the collapsed building.

Jason asked Matt to return to the Hawk residence, get all tools he could find, load them into his truck and come back to the kayak center as soon as possible.

As Matt was loading chain saws, axes, shovels, and other tools, Captain Jim and Jason began searching the heavily damaged kayak center.

Three victims had found safety under doorways in the building. Within a few minutes these three had been rescued. A fourth victim, a young woman from Portland,

Oregon, was trapped under a fallen beam that had severely cut her leg.

Matt returned with his truck and tools. Captain Jim started the chain saw. He cut the beam on either side of the victim's injured leg. The three friends carefully lifted the victim from the wreckage. She was bleeding from a severe laceration on her left leg.

Jason was trained in first aid. He applied a compression bandage. He attempted to stop blood loss. Captain Jim said it looked as if a femoral artery had been cut. If rescuers could not find a way to stop the rapid blood loss, the young kayaker might die before help could arrive. Jason tied a tourniquet that slowed the blood loss slightly but not enough.

Matt called the Coast Guard station at Port McNeill. He was told there were victims in many locations. It might be hours before help could be sent to Telegraph Cove.

Matt explained to the Coast Guard, a victim would die within minutes if help did not arrive soon. There was no available medical assistance. Jason and the Hawks were frantic.

From the nearby harbor, Argonaut felt fear in his friend's mind. He reached into Jason's thoughts. The Inua asked Jason to think about his grandfather and father.

"Remember stories of your family of Blood-Stoppers," Argonaut told his friend.

Jason froze for just a moment. He remembered stories of his ancestors being healers. Legends say that Blood-Stoppers would place one hand below the wound and one hand above the cut. With full force of his mind and heart, Jason concentrated on stopping blood flow from the wound. At first there was no change. Then, almost as if by miracle, the blood flow slowed and then stopped.

Argonaut reached out to his friend and told Jason he was also an Inua. Jason responded that he may be a Blood-Stopper but he was not an Inua.

Argonaut reached into the injured young lady's mind and calmed her. Argonaut promised her that she was safe. He told her that help would be there soon.

Within an hour, the Medivac Helicopter arrived from Nanaimo and air lifted the injured lady to the trauma center for treatment.

Before she was lifted into the flying ambulance she whispered to Jason, "You saved my life. I am forever in your debt. Whose voice did I hear calming me as you were stopping the blood flow?"

Jason said, "We just got lucky today. Come back to Telegraph Cove when you are better. We'll go kayaking together. There was no voice, I think you were in shock. You just imagined you heard someone talking to you."

Matt asked Jason how he was able to stop the girl's bleeding.

"I am the oldest son of Blood-Stoppers. We are from New Brunswick. My mother saw my Grandfather save the life of someone who was badly hurt in a fall. I remembered the story, closed my eyes, and it sort of just happened. I cannot explain it," Jason said.

"Until today I had never used this gift. I hope I never have occasion to try again," Jason said with his trembling voice.

"I had that young women's life in my hands. If I had failed, she would have died. Let's keep this story among the three of us," Jason said.

Matt stared at his friend then laughed. "Between you and Argonaut I feel like I am surrounded by the witches of Salem," Matt said.

Jason explained how Argonaut had helped by calming the young victim. The three friends began helping other volunteers clean up debris at the kayak center.

Mary Hawk brought soup and sandwiches to rescuers and survivors. It had been a difficult and scary time in Telegraph Cove. The whale museum and other buildings had a few broken windows but damage was minimal.

Other buildings had been shaken and many objects thrown off shelves. Remarkably, only the kayak center was destroyed.

The quake had registered 5.3 on the Richter Scale. Fortunately, the northern end of Vancouver Island is sparsely populated. Thankfully, no tsunami stuck the island. Tsunamis often accompany earthquakes that occur near water.

What Jason did not know, was during the quake many tons of rock had fallen over the entrance to the ancient Inuit cavern he had visited with Argonaut and Raven. Secrets that lay within the cave would forever be untouched by humans. The stone that Raven and Argonaut had moved, to open the cave, could no longer be moved. History, although wrong, would not be rewritten. The Inuit serpentine whale sculpture, Raven gave to Jason, would be the only piece of Inuit art ever found in western Canada.

CANADA AND THE PIRATES

I n Vancouver, the pirates who had taken Angel were still being interviewed by Canadian authorities. Both pirate ships involved in kidnapping Angel had been towed to Vancouver after being disabled by sharks, orcas, and dolphins. The ships were tied to docks at the Coast Guard station. Pirate ships were impounded until further notice.

Captains of both ships explained to Royal Canadian Mounted Police (RCMP), they were hired by someone in Panama to motor ships to Vancouver Island. They received instructions about kidnapping a humpback from the straits of Vancouver.

The pirates were offered a large sum of money if they would kidnap a whale and deliver it to a large container ship.

Canadian officials discovered the ships were

registered to a corporation formed on Grand Cayman Island. There was no way to trace actual masterminds of the hijack attempt. The Caymans are often used as a base for nefarious groups that want to hide their founders and owners from regulatory and taxing authorities.

Canadian Coast Guard applied for legal title to the ships. The seizure and transfer applications were granted by the British Columbia court system.

Pirates were charged with violating Canadian air and water territory, theft of Canadian marine life, and sailing with falsified papers.

The Panamanian government sent a representative to Vancouver to negotiate a resolution of the affair. Government officials of Panama offered to repay all costs of rescue operations to Canada and United States. Pirates would be prosecuted by the court system of Panama.

As is true of many other countries, there is a fair-trade agreement between Canada and Panama. The Panama Canal is essential for free-flow of products to and from Canada. If the Panama Canal were unavailable then ships would have to sail around the southern tip of South America to reach Canada. The Canadian Premier and President of Panama agreed to meet at United Nations headquarters in New York City in three days' time. They would discuss final resolution of Panamanian pirate capture of a whale and invasion of Canadian territory.

When officials from both governments met in New York, they agreed to terms of a settlement. Panama would pay Canadian Government treasury a fine of one-million Canadian dollars. Two captured pirate ships would be sold for scrap by Port of Vancouver. Proceeds of the sale of the pirate vessels would be donated to the Marine Education Research Society (MERS). The United States of America would be reimbursed seven-hundred-fifty-thousand United States dollars for use of Air Force fighters and US naval support during the whale rescue operations. Panamanian officials did not admit to any wrong doing. This agreement was classified as confidential, as is true in many similar cases.

Canada agreed to release captured pirates to Panamanian authorities.

Argonaut followed interviews of the pirates by RCMP investigators. The Inua understood the terms of agreement between the two governments. Argonaut knew there was more to the story. He felt certain there was trouble in the coming days for he and his pod. The future was not clear to him, yet. Even as his Inua powers grew, he still could not see all future events. His instincts were improving, but he was not yet at full maturity as an Inua.

Several days after the agreement was signed at United Nations headquarters, Commander Mendenhall, General Lee-Pack, Colonel Choate, Captain DeFord, and Captain Waters were meeting at SEA-TAC (Seattle – Tacoma) airport. Each individual had signed a non-disclosure agreement concerning top-secret information being discussed.

The group was called to order by Jaxon Leander, head of United States National Security Agency (NSA). The NSA director is the son of Stephanie Leander, head curator of Vancouver museum operations.

Leander called the group to order.

"We have intercepted communications between North Korea and a large criminal gang operating in Panama. North Koreans are angry their ships and hired pirates were not able to capture one of Vancouver's humpbacks. What we don't understand is why foreign operatives were trying to kidnap a whale. Does anyone have any ideas?" asked the NSA officer.

Commander Mendenhall knew immediately why North Koreans tried to kidnap one of Sitka's pod. Somehow, information about Argonaut's Inua talents had been discovered.

Mr. Leander asked Captain DeFord and Captain Waters how the foreign ships had been disabled.

Both officers explained that two pirate ships had been tangled in netting and cables probably lost during a storm.

The NSA official asked Colonel Choate if she had witnessed anything usual during her reconnaissance of the area during the rescue mission.

"I saw a lot of marine life in the area. There were no humpbacks. I saw orcas, dolphins, and even a few great white sharks. The only detectable humpback whale was captive in the hold of one of the pirate ships," said Colonel Choate.

General Lee-Pack asked the NSA representative why North Koreans wanted a humpback whale.

Mr. Leander said, "All we can determine from our intercepts is they want a magic whale."

The group laughed in unison. None of them had ever seen a magic whale.

Mr. Leander specifically asked Commander Mendenhall and Captain DeFord if they had any ideas about a motive behind the capture of Angel. Both Canadian officers said they had never seen a magic whale. If there were any in Canada, they were a secret to everyone.

Commander Mendenhall had never seen a whale do magic, so technically he had never seen a magic whale. He had heard a whale speak to him using telepathy. That had to remain a secret.

After some additional questions and answers, discussions concluded and everyone returned to their stations.

Argonaut had followed the meeting by listening to Mendenhall's thoughts. As the Canadian Coast Guard commander was returning to Vancouver from SEA-TAC, Argonaut reached out and thanked the officer for protecting his secret.

The commander said to Argonaut, "You are Inua. You have helped save animal and human lives. I promise you my best efforts to help keep you and your Inua talents safe from prying eyes."

Argonaut relayed information about the conference to Jason. They both felt relieved. Argonaut's Inua secret had not been disclosed. The danger from North Korea was not over. But for now, he and his pod were safe.

A NEW PLATFORM FOR HOPE

As Project HOPE reached an ever-increasing audience, earth's climate continued to worsen. A report was released describing significant loss of ice sheets in Antarctica.

The Denman glacier has shrunk almost three miles in slightly more than twenty-two years. If this one ice sheet were to fully melt, sea levels on earth would rise more than five feet. Almost forty percent of the population of the United States of America lives in coastal areas. A five-foot rise in sea level would destroy coastal cities from New York to Miami, and from San Francisco to Seattle.

Worldwide news network CNN contacted Project HOPE directors. The internationally known broadcast company asked for a two-hour interview with HOPE directors to be held in Vancouver on August 15. Anderson Cooper would moderate the interviews. Other participants would be Greta Thunberg and Bill Gates.

Gates was the co-founder of the software company, Microsoft. He recently retired from all Microsoft activities. He was using his time and wealth to impact worldwide change though the Bill and Linda Gates Foundation.

Thunberg was the famous young Swedish activist. She recently started a youth action movement. She was demanding immediate and significant action by world leaders to save our planet from pollution and climate change.

Chief White Feather agreed to accompany six Kitasoo student Project HOPE directors to Vancouver for the CNN interview. The program was to be aired live on worldwide television.

HOPE representatives arrived in Vancouver on a flight paid for by the Gates' Foundation. Mr. Cooper met the six students. They greeted Ms. Thunberg when she arrived in Vancouver. Everyone met Mr. Gates. He is one of the richest people on earth. He and his wife are generous, thoughtful citizens who are doing tremendous good with their fortune.

Mr. Cooper explained the interview format. He made the Kitasoo young people feel comfortable. Ms.

Thunberg was a veteran of television interviews. She was not anxious about the event. Mr. Gates has been famous for decades. He had no trepidation facing cameras.

At 4 P.M. the next day, the group assembled in the local studio of the Canadian Broadcast Company (CBC) station in Vancouver. After all participants were introduced by Mr. Cooper, he asked everyone to make an opening statement.

Mr. Gates went first. He detailed many terrible effects climate change was having on food sources, water supplies, and ever-increasing temperatures.

Greta Thunberg spoke of her experience facing governmental and corporate officials. She had met incredible resistance to any change that would reduce business profits or increase taxes.

Jill White Feather spoke about her week long trip aboard Orcella 2. She and her fellow students had proven that water quality and water temperatures were rapidly changing. She spoke eloquently of fears First Nation people had of losing their homes and way of life.

Susan Standing Bear showed slides she had taken of T-Rex while breaching. She looked into the camera and asked viewers if this magnificent animal should disappear from our planet because of pollution from plastic and other careless human behavior.

Jim Wildhorse spoke next. He told the story of visiting a Spirit Bear. He explained his tribes need for Spirit Bear Lodge to be a success. If bears had no salmon to eat, they would cease to exist.

Joan Redclaw talked of changing migration habits of salmon in Vancouver Island waters. She explained, if these changes accelerate, they would affect hibernation, breeding, and successful continuation of bear species in the northwest territories.

Mary Raven explained how temperature change encouraged great white sharks to move further north. If these giant predators ever invaded the straits near Vancouver then seals, orca, and humpbacks could become extinct.

The final Kitasoo speaker was Charles Windsong. He was the youngest Kitasoo student. He spoke with great emotion and sincerity. He explained how millions of birds were disappearing, due to ever increasing heat in Canada. He was afraid the raven might disappear from their lands. If food sources became more polluted eagles, sea birds, and ravens could become extinct. Ravens were a central figure in the myths and legends of First Nation people. He reminded viewers; extinction is forever.

Mr. Cooper asked participants what people watching the broadcast could do to help save earth.

Greta said every person eligible to vote, should register and exercise their right to vote. She asked the viewers to please vote for climate conscious officials. Only through political change could corporations be forced to stop dangerous acts of pollution.

Mr. Gates said even small changes by many people could make huge differences. Walk more, drive less. Waste less food and water. Recycle, conserve energy, develop green technologies. Many different large and small ideas were discussed.

Two hours of interviews and discussion flew by. Mr. Cooper addressed viewers and asked them to listen to what these world climate change activists had said. The words of a young Swedish student, Bill Gates, and directors of Project HOPE indicated that changes were required now, before damage became irreversible.

CBC airing of the CNN interviews had huge English language countries ratings. Broadcast of the interviews was simultaneously translated into one hundred seventeen languages.

Only history will tell if these eight activists had made a difference.

Argonaut listened to thoughts of everyone on stage and explained events to Angel, Raven, and Sitka.

For the first time in his life, Argonaut was hopeful that land creatures might begin to work together to save the planet.

ANGEL IN PERIL

ARGONAUT MEETS ANOTHER INUA

One evening that summer, Argonaut was swimming patrol duty around his pod. All adult humpbacks took turns watching for boats and other dangers to Sitka's pod.

Argonaut heard a voice in his head. The quiet voice whispered, "Hello, giant Inua."

The humpback spyhopped and searched, but could see no creature other than an old raven.

Argonaut reached out using his telepathy and said, "Who is there?"

"It is I, world's oldest and wisest Inua," a voice replied.

"Where are you?" Argonaut asked.

"I am here, in a tall tree at the edge of the island," said the voice.

The voice was coming from thoughts of the nearby ancient raven.

"How can I hear you when I did not seek you out?" Argonaut asked.

"I sought you, my young Inua friend. I too am an Inua. There are only a few of us on earth. I am called Hrafn. I am the oldest Inua that has ever lived. I have seen more sunrises than any other creature. I sensed your presence. I came to find you. I have been watching and listening, as birds do," said Hrafn.

Argonaut asked Hrafn why he had come to see him.

The ancient raven said, "My time is almost done. Soon I will fly into the sky and never again be of this place. I have learned much about you. I wanted to see for myself what the largest Inua looked like. You are a big creature," said the raven.

"I am big, but I cannot fly like you. I hope there are things you can teach me about being an Inua," Argonaut said.

"You are learning more every day. Your seeing into the future is getting clearer. You have always acted in a pure and honest way. You are already a great Inua. Your life has just begun. You have much good left to do," said Hrafn.

"I have come to warn you. I see two dangers in your future that you cannot yet see. One will be another attack on your pod. This threat will come before ten more sunrises. A long boat will come into your strait from beneath the waves of the ocean. The boat will have weapons to use in an attempt to kill a whale from your pod. A second danger will be several seasons from now. You will be hurt. You may die," Hrafn said with great sadness.

Argonaut asked if Hrafn knew these things to be true or if future events could be changed.

The raven responded that all things can change, but he was certain Argonaut's pod would be attacked soon. The raven was convinced Argonaut would be hurt, within two summer seasons.

Argonaut asked if he could stop the attack on his pod. Hrafn said, with help from Jason and his friends, the attack could be stopped. Hrafn told Argonaut that a metal ship would try to enter the Johnstone Strait and kill one of Sitka's pod.

"Why are we being targeted for death?" Argonaut asked Hrafn.

"An evil man who lives in a country far away is angry that he could not keep Angel after she was captured. He is a dangerous being," Hrafn told Argonaut.

Argonaut listened carefully to the ancient Inua. He thanked him for his warnings.

"Where will you go when your days are over?" asked the humpback.

"I will fly skyward until I am no more. My being, like all Inua, will return to the Great Spirit in the highest skies," Hrafn said.

"I have never met another Inua. Are we good or bad Inua?" asked the young whale.

"We were sent by a Great Spirit to do good. I have spent many seasons trying to help people of this land. My figure is on the poles land creatures carve. I helped them hunt. I helped them find fish. I brought them good luck. You are also here to help. You saved your pod from pods of attacking orcas. You saved your home from great white sharks. You helped a young sick humpback whale. You have done much for such a young Inua. There is much more for you to do. I see hope for a long and wonderful life for you, but there is danger. You need your human friends to help with the impending attack on your pod. When you are hurt, only they will be able to help you," Hrafn said.

Argonaut looked at the old raven and watched as he flew high into the night sky. Finally, Argonaut saw, a bright light, like a falling star, as Hrafn returned to the Great Spirit.

Argonaut felt strangely more at peace after meeting another Inua. Until now, he had felt a great burden in being Inua but Hrafn had shown Argonaut what good an Inua could do. He knew the ancient bird was wise. Argonaut began planning for the attack on his pod by an underwater boat.

ATTACK

The government of North Korea is under direct control of Kim Jong Un. His iron-fisted rule is a great risk to civilization. North Koreans are developing nuclear and ballistic weapons. People of North Korea are starving while their leader is considered a pariah by much of the civilized world. The North Korean dictator controls all aspects of life in his country.

When Kim Jong Un was told his plan to kidnap a whale from Canada had failed, he was furious. He ordered his military leaders to develop a plan to kill a whale in the straits near Vancouver. If North Koreans could not steal a whale, then they would kill one.

North Korean naval officers developed a plan. An unmanned submarine would be launched from a ship in the Pacific Ocean. The sub would navigate underwater to Johnstone Strait. The remote-controlled sub was equipped with two torpedoes to kill one or more humpback whales. There was a video link between the sub and the mother ship so operators good see a whale to target. Once a whale or whales had been killed, the unmanned submarine would return to the base ship stationed in international waters.

The North Korean unmanned sub had been tested for several months in preparation for use as a weapon of destruction. It had sophisticated sonar, radar, telemetry, heat sensors, live video capability, and advanced weapons.

Canada has no submarines and no navy. There were no underwater detection devices in the straits of Vancouver.

South Korea shares a disputed boundary with North Korea. These two nations had once been a single country. South Korea military intelligence had infiltrated the highest ranks of North Korean government and military offices.

As soon as the submarine attack plan was adopted, a South Korean agent working as a spy in the north, sent an encrypted message to the capital city of Seoul, South Korea. The spy informed South Korean military officials that North Korea was going to attack whales in the straits near Vancouver.

South Korea shared this intelligence with United Sates military officials and Canadian governmental leaders.

General Lee-Pack of the US Air Force received orders from the US Department of Defense to help Canadians protect their territory. Lee-Pack was told that under no circumstance should US military forces engage in a hostile action against North Korea forces unless it was in self-defense.

General Lee-Pack discussed the impending attack with Canadian Premier Guyaen. Canadian officials contacted Commander Mendenhall. They asked him to work with General Lee-Pack to develop a plan to keep British Columbia whales safe without provoking an international incident.

"Rene, it is Bill Mendenhall. How are you?" the Canadian Coast Guard officer asked.

"I would be a lot better if we did not have to worry about North Korean submarines invading North American waters," said General Lee-Pack.

"We do not have necessary resources to stop an unmanned sub from attacking our whales. We desperately need your help," said the Canadian commander.

"Bill, our South Korean allies have given us a lot of information. We know date and time of attack. Point of entry will be the northern terminus of Johnstone Strait. We also know which radio frequency will be used to direct the unmanned sub from a base ship in international waters," said Lee-Pack.

"What is your plan? What can we do to help?" asked Wild Bill.

"Move all humpback whales to a safer southern area. Keep them there for the duration of our joint operation," said the US general.

"I have a good friend (Argonaut) who can move whales for as long as necessary," Mendenhall said.

"Do you remember Colonel Choate, our flight squadron commander?" asked General Lee-Pack.

"I remember her well. Is she part of your plan?" asked Mendenhall.

"She is one of the main characters in our plan. She will be flying her plane, Relentless, at fifteen-thousand feet above the unmanned submarine when it crosses into Canadian waters. Her F-35 is equipped with our most modern signal jamming capability. As soon the sub crosses into your area, she will activate her jamming device. Her signal will prohibit directions from being received by the unmanned sub. Our source tells us once the submarine losses signal it will self-destruct within thirty minutes. Self-destruction is designed to stop a North Korean sub from falling into hands of another country. Having a foreign sub within another country's water is an act of war. No sane government, even that of Kim Jong Un, wants to start a war. This approach will make it look as if the sub had a malfunction," said the US general.

"Is there any risk to your pilot?" asked Commander Mendenhall.

"She is aboard the best fighter plane we have. She is one of most capable pilots in the Unites States military service. She will be supported by a United States submarine stationed five miles from the expected point of entry into Canadian territory. Her plane is called Relentless for a reason. If there are any problems, if our jet is attacked, or we are otherwise provoked, our sub has orders to destroy any North Korean vessels involved in a military operation against your country," said the general.

"Understood. I will have whales moved before North Koreans attack. On behalf of all Canadians, I want to thank you for what your country is doing to help us," said Commander Mendenhall.

"You are welcome, Bill. I will keep in touch as events unfold. I expect the enemy sub to cross Canadian maritime border within forty-eight hours. Our submarine will be able to detect the Korean vessel long before it reaches your coast. Colonel Choate will be airborne two hours before expected contact. We will have a refueling tanker flying twenty miles to her south in case there are any delays and she needs more flight time," said General Lee-Pack.

Commander Mendenhall contacted Jason. He explained how intercept of the dangerous unmanned submarine was going to occur. He instructed Jason to have Argonaut move his pod as far south as possible. Once danger has been eliminated, humpback whales could return to their sanctuary.

Jason reached out to Argonaut. He explained the plans to his Inua friend. Argonaut immediately asked Sitka to begin moving their pod south. Argonaut told his pod what was happening. He told humpbacks not to worry because his land creature friends would save them from harm.

Colonel Choate was in flight two hours before the expected violation of Canadian waters. She maintained her altitude at fifteen thousand feet. She received a communication from a US submarine that detection of a

North Korean vessel, approaching Vancouver Island, has been verified.

The F-35 pilot activated her jamming equipment as soon as the enemy sub crossed the territorial boundary of Canada. Immediately, North Korea's sub stopped all forward motion. The submarine settled to the ocean bottom.

Exactly thirty minutes after the sub's radio receiving frequency was jammed, two torpedoes aboard the enemy sub exploded. The unmanned vehicle was destroyed. There was no harm to any marine life.

Colonel Choate returned aboard Relentless to Seattle. After landing, Colonel Choate provided video proof of the subs self-destruction. The US Navy sub also confirmed recordings of an explosion.

United States officers contacted Commander Mendenhall. They told him danger to British Columbia whales had been eliminated. It was safe for whales to return home.

Events relating to the foreign invasion of Canadian territory had been classified "Top Secret". No reporting of military actions would be made public.

Argonaut called out to Commander Mendenhall. He thanked him for the intervention that saved his pod.

North Koreans never knew about the spy in their midst. No further attempts to kidnap or harm humpbacks whales were made by North Korea.

SILENT JOURNEY TO FOREVER

Life returned to normal for the Vancouver humpbacks. Their usual routine of eating, swimming, and singing helped Sitka's pod to relax. Singing is very important to humpbacks. Humans also love to sing. Humans have developed many instruments and devices to make sounds. Humpbacks are famous for their long songs. Humpback vocalizations can carry for miles underwater.

Humpbacks only have their voices to make sounds. Love songs, sounds of warning, and location sounds are all part of humpback vocal capabilities.

Humpbacks, like humans, have unique sounds when they are sad. As Sitka's pod was swimming near Telegraph Cove there was a great sound of sorrow heard from another group of whales.

Raven asked his father what the whales were sad about.

Argonaut told his son this was a song about death.

The oldest humpback matriarch, among whales living in Vancouver Island area waters, had just died at age seventy-nine. She was one of the longest living whales in memory.

Jason and Dr. Skip Foster had been called to a beach, not far from Klemtu, where the dead whale was located.

Dr. Foster took samples of the whale's organs, tissue, and blood as Jason assisted.

The whale had been named June, because that was the month she was first spotted.

Dr. Foster told Jason, "I will have a pathology lab run tissue and blood samples for analysis, but I see no visible injuries. I am fairly certain June simply died of old age."

Jason agreed and both returned to Port Hardy aboard Sadie Princess.

Argonaut heard songs of death from June's pod. He asked whales of June's pod if he could help. New matriarch of June's pod, explained that June had wanted to rest forever among ancients, in the secret whale burial cavern. She was not able to reach that sacred cave before death took her.

Argonaut used his Inua voice to call T-Rex.

Soon T-Rex joined Argonaut. Argonaut told Sitka that he and T-Rex were going to take June to their ancient burial site. Sitka gave her permission. Both large male whales went to where June was laying.

Argonaut asked Jason if he would return to where June lay as soon as possible. Jason agreed to return once Dr. Foster was at Port Hardy.

Argonaut, T-Rex, and Jason arrived at June's death site. Argonaut explained his plan to Jason.

"We need your help to arrange a rope we can use to tow June to our sacred whale burial grounds. Will you help us?" asked Argonaut.

Jason took a three-hundred-foot nylon rope from the bow of his boat. He tied a line around June and attached it to her pectoral fins. He made a loop long enough for Argonaut and T-Rex to pull June while swimming side by side.

Argonaut, T-Rex, and Jason, using Sadie Princess, turned June around so two large male humpbacks could tow June's body to her final resting place.

Argonaut thanked Jason and said, "We are going to a place not even you can go. It is a sacred burial cave unknown to humans. I will reach out to you when we return to Telegraph Cove. Please disable all tracking devices on my entire pod until I return. We are in no danger now," Argonaut said.

Jason agreed to Argonaut's request. He turned Sadie Princes towards Port Hardy. He disabled all humpback tracking devices.

Both large humpbacks took a piece of rope loop in their mouth and began the long journey to the sacred whale burial site. Argonaut had visited this site on his quest with Raven. Both T-Rex and Argonaut had also visited the site with their fathers when they went on their quests many years earlier.

June's body weighed more than fifty-thousand pounds. Argonaut and T-Rex swam in rhythm. Both humpbacks swam, steadily pulling, using their flukes to push themselves.

It was midnight when the two whales began their solemn journey with June's body in tow. They pulled June's body all night.

The humpbacks were exhausted. Their mouths were sore when sunrise occurred. They were still hours away from the sacred burial cavern.

Argonaut felt other creatures approaching. He told T-Rex to stop. Raven swam up to his father. Guardian was with Raven.

"What are the two of you doing here? How did you find us?" Argonaut asked.

"I am your son. I remember all that you have taught me. You brought me on a quest to the sacred burial site. I knew where you would be. Sitka gave us permission to help, if we could. Guardian and I will pull while you and T-Rex feed and rest," Raven told his father.

Argonaut had never felt such pride in his son and their friend Guardian.

As T-Rex and Argonaut dropped the rope loop, Raven and Guardian started pulling June towards her final resting place.

In a few minutes, six more humpbacks joined the group. New arrivals wanted to honor the late matriarch. They swam in formation behind Raven and Guardian.

Once the humpback whales entered Pacific Ocean waters, they were joined by five great white sharks.

The eldest shark asked Argonaut for permission to swim with the whales. Argonaut was moved by the gesture of respect. He accepted the great whites as part of the procession.

Soon sharks, orcas, white-sided dolphins, and birds of every species found near Vancouver Island, were moving together towards the deep burial grounds.

More whales took turns pulling June's body. At noon, they arrived at the sacred cave.

Argonaut turned towards all creatures who came to honor a fallen humpback matriarch.

Argonaut said, "You honor humpbacks by being here. We have made friends in the sanctuary. We have helped each other. Today you bring great honor to my kind. Thank you."

Orcas, dolphins, sharks, and birds all returned to their homes. Argonaut and T-Rex grabbed the rope loop. The two whales dove to the cavern entrance with June's body. Twenty whales made their entrance into the sacred cave.

Raven and Guardian removed the rope from around June's pectoral fins.

Argonaut sang, solo first, then all other whales joined him in a whale farewell song. These creatures had seen birth, sickness, death, war with other animals, and now peace. History of humpbacks is littered with stories of hunts and slaughter. Today was a day for celebrating life's end. June was now with her ancestors. She would forever rest here in peace. Whales sang for more than an hour.

Finally, Argonaut signaled his friends it was time to leave. After one final look at June, the whales returned to their homes. Humpbacks were not sad. Death is part of life's cycle. It is written, there is a time for all seasons. A time to laugh and a time to cry. There is a time to live and a time to die. June led a long and full life. She had been an honorable and respected matriarch. In the world of humpbacks, her life was one to be remembered. Her story would be told by many future generations of memory keepers

As whales entered Johnstone Strait, great whites who had been waiting for the whales to return, said goodbye and went deep into Pacific Ocean depths.

Dolphins and orcas also returned to their homes. Soon T-Rex left as quietly as he had arrived. He was still a very solitary being. Raven, Guardian, and Argonaut met their pod in a bay near Biggs Island.

Argonaut told his pod of their journey to the ancient whale burial ground. The entire pod sang their goodbye to June.

Sunset that night seemed more brilliant than usual. Stars appeared to shine more clearly. It may have been their imagination. Many whales thought they saw a new star, above the straits where June had lived her long and happy life.

RAVEN AND BIGGSY

Peace and quiet returned to Johnstone Strait. Sitka and her pod were rested, well fed, and happy. One day Raven approached his father and asked, "Father, how will I know which whale should be my mate?"

Argonaut already knew what his son really wanted to ask. He was patient with Raven.

"Son, when you find the right female to be your mate, you will be certain. You will have no doubt. You will be willing to die for her. You will want to be with her all of your days and nights. You will want her to be mother of your calves," Argonaut said.

"I want Biggsy to be my mate. I have known that since the day you and our human friends saved her," Raven said.

"Have you asked if she is willing to be your mate?" Argonaut said to his son.

"Yes. She is willing to live with me for the rest of our lives," Raven said.

Argonaut slowly approached his son. They touched noses, as whales do.

"You both have my approval for this union," father told son.

Argonaut asked his son to go tell Angel his news. Raven swam off to find his mother. Argonaut was happy for his son and Biggsy. He felt certain their lives would be long and happy.

Angel approached Argonaut. She said, "Our son may one day be a father. I hope he is as kind, thoughtful, and caring as you have been to our son."

"I think having you for a mother has made him a brave, thoughtful, considerate, and wonderful humpback," Argonaut told his mate.

Soon Sitka's entire pod knew that Raven and Biggsy were to be partners for life. Songs of joy and celebration lasted all day and well into night.

It is a secret tradition, among humpback whale pods, that each whale brings a gift to males and females who have become partners.   Shells, colored rocks, and seaweed necklaces were given to Raven and Biggsy.

Mother Biggsy was very happy for her daughter. She remembered how Argonaut, Jason, and other land creatures had saved her daughter. She was proud she and Biggsy were part of Sitka's pod.

Mother Biggsy asked Sitka if Raven and her daughter could continue to live with her pod.

"Raven and Biggsy are from different pods so their joining is accepted. They are our family.   They, like you, will always be welcome here. Perhaps, one day, Biggsy may become matriarch of this pod," said Sitka.

"Thank you for accepting us. We are both very happy to be with you," said Mother Biggsy.

It was early September when Raven and Biggsy agreed to be partners. Nights were longer. Water was colder.   Aspen leaves were changing to show winter rainbows of color. Soon it would be time for Sitka's pod to begin annual migration to warmer waters near Hawaii.

Argonaut and Angel were happy for their son. Argonaut told his mate that he saw many years of joy in their son's future. I think soon, we will be grandparents.

THE STORY OF T-REX

At sunrise the next day, Argonaut sensed a whale approaching. He knew it was T-Rex. The great solitary whale had never approached Sitka's pod unless asked. T-Rex had helped other humpbacks fight orcas. He had been a significant factor in the defense of their sanctuary against intrusion by great white sharks.

Argonaut reached out with his thoughts and said, "Hello, friend. I am glad to see you."

Argonaut immediately sensed a loneliness in T-Rex that was deep and painful.

Argonaut asked T-Rex to swim with him. Perhaps they could become better acquainted. T-Rex agreed to swim with the Inua. Both humpies swam in unison north towards Haida Gwaii.

"I can feel a deep sadness in you. Do you want to tell me why you are such a solitary whale?" asked Argonaut.

"Do you know the story of my life?" T-Rex asked Inua Argonaut.

"I know you have lived here for many years. I asked you for help with orcas, great whites, and to help take June to our sacred burial cavern. Every time you appeared and stood by my side. I think of you as a great friend," said Argonaut.

"I am lonely. I see you with your son, your mate, and your pod. I realize how sad I am being alone. I want to be like you," said T-Rex.

"You are a handsome whale. Many females would be very happy to be your partner. Why have you chosen to be alone?" Argonaut asked.

"I will tell you my life's story. I was born far away, where it is always cold. There is ice year-round where I lived. Food was plentiful. When I was less than two seasons old my parents were killed by a large ship. First, my mother was badly hurt. When my father tried to save her, he died by her side. Suddenly, I was alone. I had no pod. There were no other whales to help me. I started swimming towards the brightest star in the sky. I swam through storms, always heading towards the bright star. I was chased by orcas. Do you see the scars on my fluke? I was almost killed. I was young and afraid. I learned to be alert and careful. I hid when other whales, sharks, orcas, or land creatures came near.

One day a raven flew over my head and spoke to me as you do. His name was Hrafn. He told me he was Inua and wanted to help me. He taught me where there was good fishing. He helped me avoid orcas and sharks.

Over time, with his help, I became the biggest and strongest humpback in the ocean. Hrafn was the only creature I ever trusted, until I met you. I feel the same power and kindness in you that I felt in Hrafn.

Not long ago, Hrafn said it was time for him to go to the Great Spirit. He said I should go to the Inua Argonaut and seek his advice. I needed no other creature when Hrafn was near. Now that he is gone, I feel as lonely as I did when I was a young calf.

I was bullied, beat up, alone, and afraid. The only creatures that ever cared about me were killed. I had to learn to be by myself. No other pod offered to help, so I became a lonely sad whale. Because of my size and strength, I am no longer afraid of any creature. I am tired of being alone. Can you help me?" T-Rex asked Argonaut.

"My friend that is a very sad story. No whale should be left as an orphan when so young. I have always been part of a pod. I have never felt as lonely and sad like you. I think there is something we can do. I want you to stay very still. Hold your fins straight out from your side. Close your eyes and listen to my voice in your thoughts. Will you do that?" Argonaut asked.

T-Rex did as he was asked. Argonaut reached deep into his thoughts. Argonaut felt deep pain and sadness in T-Rex's life. It made Argonaut very sorry for his friend. He told T-Rex, what happened so many years ago was long past. Argonaut said he would take the pain from T-Rex's heart. Soon T-Rex would find peace. With the depth of his Inua powers, Argonaut willed T-Rex's pain to disappear. Inua powers let Argonaut slowly release the pain from T-Rex's mind and heart.

As they were floating, side by side, T-Rex felt a great weight lifted from his heart and mind. He opened his eyes. He looked at Argonaut.

"You are my friend. I am forever in your debt. You have given me hope. May I ask you another question?" said T-Rex.

Argonaut said, "I can read you mind. The answer is yes. You can join our pod. We will be your family. You will never be alone again. I happen to know that Mrs. Biggsy thinks you are a brave and wonderful whale. She does not have a mate. Perhaps the two of you may find happiness together."

T-Rex was so happy he breached again and again. Both whales sang happy songs. They returned to Angel, Raven, Biggsy, and Mrs. Biggsy. It was the happiest day ever for T-Rex.

MARINE EDUCATION RESEARCH SOCIETY

J ason and other volunteers with Marine Education Research Society (MERS) had been busy all spring and summer. The group was wisely spending funds received from sale to the Vancouver Art Museum of an Inuit serpentine humpback sculpture given to Jason by Raven. Jason had saved Raven's life after being trapped in a large net.

MERS sponsored a large gathering of local First Nation tribes at Hakai Recreation area. Events at the gathering included games, lectures, and seminars about local wildlife. Food was brought by each tribe to share. Stories were told around campfires.

MERS sponsored a wood carving contest among local tribes. All carvings were offered for sale on the MERS website to help raise funds to support efforts of Project HOPE.

Jason, Matt, and Captain Jim gave tours aboard both Orcella 2 and Sadie Princess. Kitasoo guides took small groups to see a Spirit Bear. Many First Nation members had never seen a Spirit Bear. Matt had hydrophones hooked to a loud speaker so whales, orcas, and dolphins could be heard.

The event was a success. Everyone promised to make gathering at Hakai an annual event.

Jason and other volunteers were presenting seminars on whale safety in Vancouver, Victoria, Nanaimo, Port McNeill, and Port Hardy. MERS posted more than one-hundred "See a Blow, Go Slow" signs in Alert Bay, near Duke Point, in Departure Bay, and other areas of the Strait of Georgia and Johnstone Strait.

Captain Jim met with officials of the British Columbia Ferry Company and reached an agreement. Ferries would be more careful in areas where whales and other marine life congregated.

Jason and Matt attended a convention in Vancouver, for cruise ship operators. They told the group about dangers to wildlife from pollution and boat strikes. Jason explained if cruise ship operators agreed to slow down their ships in the Vancouver area straits, then passengers might have a better chance to see and photograph orcas, whales, and dolphins. Jason promised if ships were more careful, more animals would appear for passengers to see. Argonaut had already asked his marine friends to be more visible, if ships were more cautious.

Captain Jim, Matt, and Jason did a series of one-day education trips aboard Orcella 2 for young Kitasoo Xai'xais students. Trips aboard Orcella 2 were always popular with youngsters from Klemtu.

Jason was interviewed for a Project HOPE YouTube broadcast. He spoke with passion about ever-increasing water temperatures, plastic waste pollution, and changing migration patterns of salmon. Bear hibernation activity was changing, as a result of climate change.

MERS started a "SPONSOR A WHALE" program. Individuals and businesses could sponsor a whale. In exchange for their donation, donors would receive a picture of the whale, as well as a fact sheet about humpback whales. Argonaut, T-Rex, Angel, and Guardian were part of the adopt a whale program.

MERS also held a silent auction. Bidders could log onto the MERS website and bid on donated items. Jason donated many beautiful pictures of wildlife for sale in the auction. Captain Jim and Matt offered for bids, three one-day tours aboard the Orcella 2. Mary Hawk had written a children's book. She gave five autographed copies of the book to MERS for the auction. The event raised over seven-thousand dollars for MERS projects.

HUMPBACK BEHAVIOR

As fall was ending, it was time for the humpbacks to begin their migration to Hawaiian waters. The journey was more than twenty-seven hundred miles. Often there were storms, floating debris and ships to avoid. Both Jason and Argonaut knew it was nearing migration time for Sitka's pod.

Jason asked the Inua how whales knew when it was time to migrate. Jason also asked how whales could navigate such a vast distance without getting lost.

Argonaut thought about his answer and said, "We have to migrate because young calves do not have enough fat to survive in the cold winters of our sanctuary. They are born in our winter home, get stronger, then return in spring when water here is warmer. We have always traveled to warmer waters in winter. It is part of humpback behavior. It is nothing that we have to think about, it is natural. Sitka has told me stories of other whales that migrate more than twice as far as we do. She told me of butterflies that migrate over land they have never seen. I think we learn the routes from matriarchs of each generation. Legend has stories of salmon migrating based on smell of the river where they were born. We migrate because it is what we know how to do. It is what we have always done, since the beginning of time."

"Do you talk to other whales as you migrate?" Jason asked the Inua.

"We often speak to other pods. We know how much further we have to go by what other pods say," Argonaut replied.

"It seems a remarkable feat to cross almost three-thousand miles of water and arrive at exactly the right place ever year. You have no tools or modern devices," Jason said.

"I think there are other parts to the puzzle of our migration that you do not understand. We often spyhop when the sky is dark and look at the brightest stars to know where we are. In our thoughts, there is an inner voice that helps guide us. I do not understand how the inner voice guides us, but it does," Argonaut said.

"I have read that magnetic forces may affect migratory behavior of many creatures, even humpbacks. I am not sure, since you are the first whale that has ever talked to a human. Do you understand what I mean by magnetic field?" Jason asked.

"I can read you mind and understand what you think. I can see what you see. I hear what you hear. I am Inua. That is a big help in learning and understanding. However, I am not human. There will always be differences between us, just as there are between orcas, dolphins, sharks, and humpbacks," Argonaut said.

"Biggsy and Raven are now partners. T-Rex has joined our pod. Mother Biggsy has agreed to be his partner. Angel will have another calf when we are in our winter home. I may soon be a grandfather, if Raven and Biggsy have a son or daughter. Being an Inua is hard. I listen to so many thoughts that I often cannot rest. I try to take away pain. I seek out peace, when sometimes I would rather be angry and fight. I know it is important that you and other land creatures change the world so the waters get clean, temperatures do not increase, and life can continue. I worry that I may not be able to help save our world," Argonaut told Jason.

"Humans are often not kind or gentle. We sometimes neglect the most important things due to greed. Kitasoo students of Project HOPE, and others like them around the world, are trying to make a difference. What does your Inua instinct tell you of the future?" Jason asked.

"I see hope. I see danger. I know you and I will always be friends. I see that together we will do as much good as we can," the Inua said.

"I hope you and your pod have a safe journey. I will wait for you to return home in the spring. Be very careful. Our world needs the great Inua Argonaut," Jason said.

Argonaut reached out his pectoral fin so Jason could touch him before the whales left.

Argonaut rejoined the pod. The group started their long swim to Hawaii.

WINTER, A TIME OF CHANGE

In early November, after the Sitka pod left for Hawaii, the Hawk family delivered Orcella 2 to a shipyard in Vancouver. Jason followed the Hawks to Vancouver aboard Sadie Princess. Orcella 2 and Sadie Princess both needed a hull scrape and paint job. Even in cold waters of northwest Canada, barnacles form on boat hulls. Boats need periodic scraping and painting.

The three Hawks parted ways at Vancouver airport. Matt headed to Australia to film a documentary for the British Broadcasting Company about ongoing pollution damage to the great barrier reef. Matt was working with Emmy award winning documentary film maker, Blair Foster of New York. Blair is the daughter of Dr. Skip Foster, the marine veterinarian, who saved Biggsy last year. Jason caught a ferry ride back to Port Hardy.

Jim and Mary Hawk flew to Key West, Florida for three months of warm sunshine. During their stay, they rested from their busy summer tour season in Telegraph Cove.

Jason had several articles to write for National Geographic Magazine, Canadian Outdoor Magazine, and other publications. Jason also promised Professor John Leibach to spend two weeks as a guest lecturer at the marine biology department at University of Alaska Southeast, in Juneau, Alaska. Professor Leibach is chairman of the marine biology department. Professor Leibach and Jason have known each other for many years. They have worked together on numerous projects and articles.

Leibach was a world-renowned expert on marine life. Jason was a prominent researcher. Jason was a published writer in the field of whales, orcas, and dolphins. Jason's photos were often used by Professor Leibach's students as part of their course work.

One issue being discussed in Professor Leibach's graduate course on marine biology, was the viability of animal-to-human organ transplantation. Pigs have a similar genetic structure to humans. Work was being done to see if pigs could be genetically engineered, so organs could be procured from pigs and transplanted into a human body. Experimentation with pig organs and transplantation into baboons is currently underway. Baboons are very close biological relatives to humans.

Human organ donation and transplantation is a major medical procedure. Many humans die each year because of insufficient donor organs available when needed. Animal-to-animal donation was being studied to understand if, one day, animal-to-human donation could occur. If animals could be used as a source of organs, then many human deaths could be avoided.

Jason did not know then, but in the near future there would be a terrible disaster in the straits of Vancouver. A major animal-to-animal organ donation would be attempted in Vancouver waters.

The Leviathan, a whale watching tour boat operation, was idle during the winter. In November, the Telegraph Cove whale museum closed for the season. Transient orcas left for warmer waters. Resident orcas remained in the straits of Vancouver. Like humpbacks, resident orcas lived off stored fat reserves. There were no salmon in the area during the coldest months of the year.

Temperatures often dropped below freezing in the far Pacific Northwest. Snow was relatively common. Waters of the straits near Vancouver Island did not freeze because of high salt content of the water and heavy tidal flows.

Bears were in hibernation. Eagles were more abundant. Harsh winters in Alaska often led eagles and other birds to fly south.

Spirit Bear Lodge was closed until Spring. Students on Klemtu had a lot of school work to finish. A provincial senior achievement test was administered in March. LeeAnne and Sarah were working, using Khan Academy, to accelerate learning for all Kitasoo students.

Project HOPE continued to demand significant time from all six directors. Letters were written. Interviews granted. Podcasts continued to be developed. Email contact with thousands of chapters was maintained.

What residents of Vancouver Island did not yet know; three new members were added to Sitka's pod during the winter. T-Rex and Mother Biggsy had a calf. He was one of the biggest calves ever born. His parents named him Little Rex.

Raven and Biggsy had a calf. She was born under a rainbow. Her pod named her Rainbow. Argonaut and Angel were now grandparents.

Angel also had a calf and he was named Jason. The whales knew the legend of Jason and the Argonauts.

Since Argonaut is named after the Argonauts of legend, it seemed appropriate, to the Inua and his mate, to name their son Jason. Another reason for the name given to Argonaut's newest son was that the Inua's best friend was Jason Belliveau. It seemed right for Argonaut and Angel to name their second son Jason. Jason had saved Raven from drowning. Jason had taught Argonaut to speak using the Underwater Wet PC.

Water was warm, whales were relaxed. They rested and enjoyed calm water surrounding the Hawaiian Islands. Young whales nursed, as all newborn mammals do. Calves grew stronger every day.

Young humpbacks were taught to sing by their parents.

Raven was excited to have a brother. He was also very proud to a first-time father. He had been an only child before Jason, the new calf, was born. Biggsy was a great mother. She was careful to protect Rainbow. She never wanted her daughter to lose Sitka's pod. Biggsy and Mother Biggsy had been separated from their own pod during a violent storm. The Sitka pod had welcomed the two lost whales into their pod. Biggsy had been saved by Argonaut and his human friends when she was very sick.

There were other pods in the waters of Hawaii. The whales were friendly and called to one another. There was harmony amongst the humpbacks.

HOMEWARD BOUND

I n early April, Sitka told her pod to prepare for their eastern migration to straits of Vancouver. Argonaut was anxious to see his friend Jason. Mature humpbacks were hungry after their long winter fast.

Crossing from Hawaii to Canada was uneventful. New calves were constantly guarded by adults. Forming a protective ring of adults around the calves, day and night, made for a safe journey. It took almost three weeks of traveling for Sitka's pod to reach Vancouver's Johnstone Strait.

Argonaut was now nine years old. He had reached his full size and strength. His Inua powers continued to grow. Often, during the trip from Hawaii, Argonaut had visions of events that would happen in his sanctuary. Inua could influence but not control future happenings. Argonaut knew he would be involved in many new adventures with Jason and his other land creature friends.

In passing, Argonaut called out to all great white sharks who lived east of Vancouver Island. The eldest shark welcomed Sitka's pod home. Argonaut asked if any shark hunters had bothered his friends. The great white shark replied, there were no hunters after last year's incident. Argonaut, Raven, and Guardian, with the help of several great whites, saved a shark caught in a net, otherwise doomed to death.

The next creatures Argonaut encountered were resident orcas who were in the area all winter. There was a new calf in the resident orca pod. He was an unusual color. The young orca was entirely white, not the usual black and white coloration of most orcas. Orcas named the young white orca, Argo, in honor of the great Inua who had made peace with orcas living in the straits near Vancouver. Argonaut was honored. He thanked all orcas for their friendship.

The first white orca was spotted in 2010 in the western Pacific Ocean. In the two decades since first discovery of a white orca, at least five others have been identified. In no other area are these white orcas found. White orca are albinos. A lack of skin pigmentation makes animals white in color. An albino animal is different than a Great Spirit Bear which is a product of recessive genes.

There was a famous albino humpback named Migaloo. Many other species also produce albinos.

When the pod reached Hanson Island, Sitka allowed her family to eat and rest. Argonaut, T-Rex, Raven, and Guardian took turns guarding the pod from dangers. Food was plentiful. Krill and herring were in abundance.

Argonaut called out to Jason. They set a time, sunrise on the following day, to meet near orca rubbing beach. Sadie Princess and Orcella 2 had both returned from dry dock. The hull of Sadie Princess was freshly painted. When the two friends met underwater, Argonaut presented his nose for Jason to touch. It was their usual way of greeting each other.

Argonaut told Jason of three calves born into Sitka's pod during the winter. Argonaut promised to bring the young calves to meet Jason, as soon as they were rested.

As spring reached Vancouver Island, ferries, cruise ships, and tourist boats became more abundant. The Leviathan resumed its twice daily tours of the marine sanctuary.

KITASOO STUDENTS GRADUATE

April 22, 2021 was National Earth Day. In honor of six Project HOPE directors graduating from Klemtu School, ceremonies were held on this year's National Earth Day. Jill White Feather was unanimously chosen by her tribe to be Valedictorian of the 2021 graduating class.

The guest speaker was Jane Goodall. Ms. Goodall is one of the most famous animal rights activists in history. She is renowned for her work with apes in Africa. Her career has spanned over six decades.

Ms. Goodall addressed the graduating class, family, and guests gathered in the Klemtu Big House. With so many guests and dignitaries in attendance a huge tent, additional seating, and two large video screens were set up outside the Big House.

Ms. Goodall rose to speak,

When I was a young girl, many years ago, animal rights were not a concern. Pollution, climate change, species extinction, and other horrors of modern life were never discussed. I began my research and learned about the great apes of Africa the same way your people have learned about marine life, Spirit Bears, and different birds of your area. It does my heart wonders to see so many active, engaged, and intelligent students involved in world affairs helping to effect change. I hope you stay committed to saving our planet in the future, as you have done since the start of Project HOPE, two years ago. You are making a difference. The fight is now yours. My time is almost at an end. I am relieved and proud the mantle is being passed to the wonderful group of Klemtu School graduates here today. Time is short. Conditions are critical. Now is not the time to relax our efforts and our vigilance. Your very lives are in the balance. Fight with all of your energies to save our planet. My hopes and prayers are with you.

After a long-standing ovation, Jill White Feather rose to speak.

Ms. Goodall, guests, families, and fellow graduates. None of us made it here today by ourselves. Our families, teachers, tutors, and friends all helped shape us. We live on a small island in an isolated rain forest. Even in this remote area, we are connected to everyone else on earth. We all breathe polluted air. We drink contaminated water. Global temperatures are rising, ice sheets are melting, animals are disappearing. If we want change, then we in this room, on this island, in this country, on our planet, all must act now. Project HOPE is making a difference. Famous people like Bill and Linda Gates, Jane Goodall, Greta Thunberg, and millions of others are working feverishly to save our planet.

We will not rest, wherever our paths may lead us. Our fight has just begun. We have fierce adversaries in large corporations that have no moral compass. Many governments are not run for the long-term welfare of their citizens, but more for special interests.

We have heard today from one of the most famous animal rights activists who ever lived. She is our role model. She is our hero. Those of us graduating today have decided to take a skip year. We will not start jobs, careers, or go to college. For the next full year, all of our eighteen graduating seniors will commit one-hundred percent of our time and energy to Project HOPE.

We are now six-million members strong, with chapters in almost every country of the world. We have not solved global warming, over population, pollution, destruction of habitat, and other issues we are working on. We are trying. With help from all members of Project HOPE, we will win the battle, because the alternative is extinction. Thank you.

A thunderous roar rose from inside the Big House and from guests seated outside. Jane Goodall walked to Jill White Feather and raised her hand into the air. The picture of the elderly animal activist and the young Kitasoo student made every news broadcast on radio and television. It was on the front cover of every newspaper in the world. Video of the event went viral. The world was on notice. Project HOPE was here to stay, here to fight, and here to win.

Some guests and out-of-town families were flown by commercial helicopter to Vancouver and Port Hardy for their return flights home. Others had come to Klemtu aboard their own boats. Many visitors boarded the BC Ferry returning to Vancouver. Commander Mendenhall had arranged a charter ferry for travel to and from Vancouver.

Jason, Matt, Captain Jim and Mary were at graduation. They were now returning to Telegraph Cove, aboard Orcella 2.

"A remarkable group of young people," said Mary Hawk.

"I am very thankful for the small part the Orcella 2, us, and MERS played in developing Project HOPE," Matt said.

"Jason, do you think there is a chance young Kitasoo students may have an impact on climate change, pollution, and other issues they are fighting?" asked Captain Jim.

"I am not sure. There is so much inertia in human behavior. It is difficult to make change, even when it is critical. Corporations, governments, religions, civic and social groups all have to get involved and fight to save earth," Jason said.

"I hope they succeed as water we see around us, beautiful animals, and our incredibly clear skies are all in danger," Matt said with a deep sadness in his voice.

Return boat ride to Telegraph Cove was quiet. Water was calm as the moon rose over Canada shining its glimmering light on bays, inlets, and forests of Johnstone Strait. Whales were blowing, birds were flying, and fish were jumping. None of the people on the boat said a word. They just enjoyed the majesty of the marine sanctuary.

SPIRIT BEAR HUNTED

Three Canadian hunters were returning from a brown bear hunt in Western Alaska. The immediate past President of the United States had expanded legal hunting of brown bears. It is legal to hunt brown and black bears, during some seasons, in certain areas of Alaska. There are strict rules about hunting bears. Tags for killed bears, licenses, permits, and a host of restrictions apply. Violating hunting rules can lead to substantial fines, forfeiture of property, and imprisonment.

In 2017, the Province of British Columbia banned trophy grizzly bear hunting. A poll showed more than ninety percent of Canadians opposed bear trophy hunting. Hunting for bear meat, as food, by First Nation tribes is still allowed, except in the Great Bear Rainforest, home of Spirit Bears.

The Canadian hunters returning from Alaska had permits to hunt brown bears in Alaska. Each of the three hunters had killed a grizzly. Conservationists and animal activists find killing bears for sport barbaric. It is roundly condemned. Despite all the criticism and disdain for hunters like these men, bear hunting is still legal.

The hunters had chartered an experimental aircraft to fly them to and from Alaska. The plane was called Dornier Seastar. The German manufactured aircraft was first certified in 2020. It is produced as part of a joint venture with Chinese manufacturers. Seastar had sufficient range to transport hunters from Vancouver to Anchorage. The plane had dual engines. It was designed for landing and takeoff on land or in water. Flight plans for returning to Canada called for a sightseeing stop in waters of the Great Bear Rainforest.

These hunters were not sightseers. Stopping in waters near Klemtu was part of a deliberate plan to shoot and skin a Spirit Bear. A Spirit Bear hide was a defining highlight of an evil illegal hunter's collection. There was no legal market for a Spirit Bear hide. These men were simply vicious, unprincipled sport killers, with no regard for the laws of Canada or the First Nation people of the area.

These three hunters were rich oil barons from Calgary. Prior to the great oil depression of 2020, each man had made more than five-hundred-million dollars, in profit, from oil and gas exploration.

In the plane's luggage compartment, were stowed three Ruger Hawkeye Alaskan model rifles. The guns had no high-end optics. To kill a bear with a single shot, it must be at close range. If you do not kill a large bear with one shot, you may not get a second chance. This rifle had iron sights for use as additional defense, if a bear charged. Each man was an expert rifleman. They killed without regard for rules and regulations.

All hunters know, the act of entering rainforest property was against Canadian and Tribal laws unless accompanied by a First Nation guide. What these hunters did not know was these waters are patrolled by drones with numerous motion-activated cameras broadcasting information to Canadian Wildlife Offices in Port McNeill. Hydrophones are placed strategically in many locations in Great Bear Rainforest area waters to detect boats and planes landing in protected areas.

As soon as the plane landed, authorities knew an unauthorized entry was being made to Kitasoo lands.

The RCMP duty staff alerted tribal police in Port Hardy. The Canadian Coast Guard was notified that trespassers had entered Great Bear Rainforest.

Once Seastar was anchored, a small inflatable raft took the trespassers from the aircraft to shore.

These three hunters were on a Spirit Bear Lodge trip last year. They knew where a mature Spirit Bear lived. As the hunters climbed a hill, they heard a helicopter approaching from the south. The three hunters turned towards the sound of the approaching helicopter. They spotted a Canadian Coast Guard helicopter. The trespassers quickly made their way back towards their raft. The helicopter hovered over the raft. A loud broadcast from the helicopter's speakers told the men to put down their weapons and raise their hands.

One of the hunter's panicked. He fired a shot at the helicopter. The bullet hit the left arm of pilot Captain Bruce Brient. His co-pilot that day was Lieutenant Commander Peggy Pierstorff. The co-pilot quickly assumed command of the aircraft.

A second shot by one of the hunters was fired. It hit the helicopter's rotor assembly causing a massive hydraulic leak. The helicopter was in serious trouble. Pierstorff had just a few moments to make a decision. She broadcast the helicopters location over the radio. She decided her only alternative as to make a dangerous beach landing.

The helicopter was flying erratically as control commands were failing, due to the hydraulic leak. Just as the rotors stopped, the co-pilot made a hard landing on a small beach with only a few inches of clearance between rotating blades and nearby trees.

Captain Brient suffered a through-and-through flesh wound. The helicopter was badly damaged. Both Coast Guard crew members were alive. Lieutenant Commander Pierstorff helped her injured friend from the wrecked helicopter. She used the first aid kit to bind the wound. Help was not far away.

On routine patrol, Canadian Coast Guard Ship CCGS Risley had seen the helicopter crash and heard the co-pilot's call for help. The Risley deployed a zodiac with three armed seamen and a medic aboard to assist the pilot and co-pilot.

After firing two shots at a Coast Guard helicopter all three hunters threw their weapons in the harbor. Three scared men tried to reach Seastar. Just as the hunters reached their aircraft, Risley fired five-hundred rounds of fifty-caliber machine gun rounds, with tracers lighting every sixth round, near the plane. Captain DeFord broadcast over the ships loudspeakers orders for the men to raise their hands. There was no choice but to surrender to Risley's superior force.

The CCGS Risley stayed close to the plane. A tribal police officer arrived at the scene by boat. The officer handcuffed each man. He put them into his boat. The tribal officer radioed the Risley and thanked Captain DeFord.

"It was our pleasure. Those idiots shot one of our Coast Guard pilots and ruined a ten-million-dollar helicopter. Where are you taking the felons?" asked Captain DeFord.

"I will leave them with the Kitasoo on Klemtu until an RCMP boat arrives. Mounties will transport these criminals to Vancouver for trial," the officer replied.

The zodiac returned from the crash site to the Risley with Captain Brient and Lieutenant Commander Pierstorff. Brient was transported to the ship's medical unit for treatment.

Pierstorff asked DeFord to leave a contingent of sailors to stand guard at the crash site. A full inquiry would be convened. Evidence must be kept uncontaminated. Captain DeFord sent four sailors back, by zodiac, to the helicopter crash area. The seamen were instructed to wait for the RCMP vessel. The Risley departed at high speed to Port Hardy where Captain Brient was able to board a plane to Vancouver, for additional medical assessment.

After the Risley departed, Argonaut swam close to where Seastar was still anchored. Inua telepathy had warned all Spirit Bears to hide in deep woods before the hunters had reached land. Spirit Bears were never in danger from the hunters. Argonaut was involved again in helping other creatures. After danger had passed, Argonaut told the bears it was safe to resume fishing, which bears are always happy to do.

Three prisoners made their first appearance before Chief Provincial Court Judge, James Nilon. The men were charged with criminal trespass on First Nation land, attempted murder of federal officers, illegal discharge of a weapon, destruction of governmental property, and attempting to evade officers.

Judge Nilon asked how the men pleaded. Three arrogant rich men assumed, because of their influence and political contributions, they would face a fine and perhaps loss of their hunting permits. Each man, against advice of personal lawyers, plead guilty.

Judge Nilon said, "Attempting to kill a Spirit Bear is a felony. Attempted murder of a federal official is a felony. Discharge of a weapon while attempting a crime is a felony. Destruction of a Coast Guard helicopter worth millions of dollars is a felony. For these crimes, I sentence each of you to five years' incarceration in Kent Institution in Agassiz, British Columbia. You are ordered to pay a fine of ten-million dollars each for helicopter destruction, costs of your capture, and penalties for your actions. Upon your release you will serve five years' probation. If you violate your probation, you will return to Agassiz for another five years of incarceration. I hereby order you to surrender your passports, driver's licenses, pilot's licenses, and hunting permits. You will never again fly an airplane or hunt an animal."

Three powerful men were stunned. They were led away from court by RCMP officers to a waiting van for transportation to the maximum-security correctional facility.

Lawyers tried to object. Chief Judge Nilon said "Case closed. File an appeal if you choose. I have made my decision."

Both Coast Guard helicopter pilots were in court when sentencing occurred. Brient and Pierstorff were satisfied with the judgement. Captain Brient returned to active duty and suffered no lasting effects from his injury.

CLIFFORD L. GIONET

WHEN EAGLES CRY

Argonaut and Angel, swimming west of Hanson Island, heard mournful cries from a bald eagle. Both whales spyhopped and saw an eagle standing on shore by the water's edge. Usually, eagles are in trees, unless hunting. They swoop down, pick up a fish or small mammal. Once they catch quarry, eagles return to their nest, often to feed their mate or offspring.

Argonaut asked the eagle why he was sad. The eagle was stunned by the voice in his head. Argonaut seemed to have that effect the first time he spoke to creatures using Inua telepathy.

"Do not be afraid. I am Argonaut the Inua. I will help you, if I can," Argonaut said.

The bird looked at both whales near the shore. He told Argonaut that he had lost his mate. Argonaut knew eagles mated for life. The Inua also knew the horror he felt when Angel was kidnapped.

"What happened to your mate?" Argonaut asked.

The eagle told his story to Argonaut who repeated it using his powers, so that Angel would understand. The two eagles had been hunting fish near a lodge on Haida Quai. Both eagles were resting on electrical wires as they scanned surrounding waters for more fish. Suddenly, as his mate spread her wings, there was a loud bang and a bright light. His mate fell from her perch on the wires to the ground. She never moved after she fell.

"Why did she fall?" asked Argonaut.

"I do not know. We sat on these same wires many times. She was wet. She spread her wings as wide as she could to let them dry. As soon as her wings were spread, she fell dead. I do not know what caused my mate to die, but I am forever lost," the bald eagle cried.

Argonaut reached out to Jason. He asked his friend to explain what had happened to the eagle's mate. Jason told Argonaut electrocution is the most common cause of death among bald eagles. A mature bald eagle has a wing span of between six and seven feet. If standing on an electrified wire and one wing touches another electric wire, or a ground, then electrocution occurs. The eagle dies from the electrical current.

Argonaut explained to Angel and the eagle what Jason had said. The eagle understood, but he was so sad he wanted to give up. He felt lost, abandoned. He did not want to live without his mate. His heart was broken. Like humans who lose a loved one, animals often feel deep sadness at the loss of a mate or offspring.

Angel urged Argonaut to help the eagle. She had known fear and loneliness when she had been kidnapped. Angel felt sorry for the lonely eagle.

Argonaut asked the eagle if he knew about Inua beings.

The eagle replied, "My species has legends of Inua, but I have never met one. According to our legends, Inua are kind, powerful, and able to see some future events before they occur. Inua can do wonderful things. I also know that not even Inua can bring back the dead."

"Do you believe in these legends of Inua?" Argonaut asked.

The eagle thought for a moment and spoke using his mind, "Since we are talking, eagle to whale, at least part of the stories must be true."

Argonaut smiled and said, "I am Inua. I am here to help you. I lost my mate for a time but, unlike you, mine was saved."

"Where do spirits of eagles go when they die?" Argonaut asked the eagle.

"Our legends say, after death, our spirits fly into the heavens. We become another star. We will shine forever. The dead will never again be hungry, cold, or suffer," the eagle replied.

"I think your legends are true. I saw an Inua raven at the time of his death. I watched his spirit fly away until a new star appeared. I think your mate is now a shining star," said Argonaut.

"I believe you, great Inua, but I am still very sad and lonely. When eagles mate, we are never apart except when we are hunting for food. My partner was with me for eight winters. I do not know how to live without her," the eagle said.

Argonaut told the eagle to close his eyes. Think of your mate in all her beautiful feathers. Argonaut told the eagle to imagine his mate flying into the darkness of night until she became a star. The eagle did as Argonaut asked. He imagined his mate flying to the heavens and becoming a star. Argonaut reached deep into the mind of the eagle.

Using his Inua powers, Argonaut took as much pain as he could from the bird. The eagle felt a sense of happiness and hope he had not felt since his mate's death.

The eagle looked at Argonaut and said, "You are a kind Inua. I thank you for helping me. I will never forget my first mate. I will always keep her in my heart. I am only ten winters old. Perhaps, someday, I will find another mate. She will not be the same as my first mate but perhaps I can be happy again. Maybe, if I find another mate, together we can start a new life."

"If I can ever help, just reach out for me. I will come. I will do whatever I can for you and your pod," the eagle told his new Inua friend.

The eagle promised to be Argonaut's friend for life.

"What is your name, my new friend?" Argonaut asked.

As the eagle started to fly away from the beach he circled. He thought to Argonaut, "My name is Nakturalik. Remember me, my Inua guardian. We will see each other again."

What Argonaut and Angel did not know was soon this eagle would be very important in their lives. The eagle flew off, high above the trees.

Angel touched her nose to Argonaut's and said, "I am proud to be your mate. You always seem to help others in need. I think you may be the greatest Inua of all time."

Argonaut said, "I hope I always make you proud."

Both whales slowly swam back to the pod deep in thought. Argonaut was continuing to have ever darkening visions cross his mind about his own future. He did not share his fears with Angel. Argonaut's flashes of his future were frightening.

YOUNG DOLPHINS LEARN A LESSON

Sitka's pod was feeding a short distance from their normal habitat because bait fish were in abundance further south. In the southern part of the marine sanctuary, resident orcas are common. These southern resident orcas do not eat meat, just fish.

Pacific white-sided dolphins seem to know which orcas are residents and which are transients. Dolphins swim in pods ranging from a few hundred to as many as a thousand different animals. Each dolphin has a unique sound.

Dolphins will swim with resident orcas. They may be protecting themselves from transients by swimming among the residents. The two types of orcas, residents and transients, avoid each other. Dolphins do not fear residents, only transients.

As the humpies were feeding, Argonaut watched a

group of young dolphins harass an older resident orca. Dolphins are very fast swimmers. An older orca is not likely to catch a faster young dolphin.

Young dolphins were actually hitting the orca with their tails, noses, and heads. The two species could not communicate. It was clear, the elder orca was disturbed by the aggressive young dolphins.

The aging orca was separated from his pod. There was no help nearby. The dolphins were not fearful of Sitka's pod because humpbacks have no teeth and they are not aggressive. The young dolphin bullies were relentlessly tormenting the old orca.

Argonaut sensed harm being done to the orca. He decided to teach the young dolphins a lesson.

He called out to T-Rex, Raven, and Guardian. Argonaut asked them to join him. They were going to surround the orca to protect him from danger. Four large humpbacks surfaced. The whales swam beside the orca. Argonaut told the orca that he and his friends were there to help. Argonaut explained to the orca that he was an Inua. These aggressive young dolphins needed to learn to respect others. Bullying was not acceptable behavior among creatures of the sanctuary.

Dolphins started another attack on the orca. Under Argonaut's guidance, all four whales breached right on top of the dolphins. The dolphins had not expected the humpbacks to get involved in their attack on the old orca. They were upset.

Argonaut could sense what the dolphins would do next. He instructed T-Rex to swim below the orca and just as the dolphins attacked again, T-Rex flipped his enormous fluke and threw three young dolphins completely out of the water.

Argonaut said to the dolphins, using his Inua powers, "That is enough. I am Inua Argonaut. This orca and all orcas are under my protection. We have made peace with the orcas. I have never had to discipline or fight dolphins, but we will protect our friends. Do you understand me?'

"We are not afraid of humpbacks," said one of the dolphins.

"We have teeth, swim faster, and there are many of us. This old orca and you four humpbacks cannot hurt us. We will do as we wish," said another young dolphin.

The Inua used his power to reach deep into the minds of the three dolphins. Argonaut froze the dolphins so they could not move. They could not swim, dive, or move a muscle.

"I will not release you unless you promise not to attack the resident orcas. You are cowards. You would never dare attack a transient who could easily kill you. We all live in the same waters. We need to help each other. Someday you will be old and slower than you are now. Like my old orca friend, you may need help. You will not want to be harassed just because you are old. Do you understand?" Argonaut said.

All three dolphins agreed to stop attacking the elder orca.

Argonaut told each of the dolphins to find a fish and bring it to the orca as an apology and sign of respect. Three humbled dolphins agreed. Argonaut released his hold on the three adolescent dolphins. Within minutes three dolphins had returned with a fish. In turn, each dolphin gave their fish to the orca.

"Go, my young dolphin friends. Live with more respect for other creatures. If you need my help simply call out using your thoughts. I and my pod will help, if we can," Argonaut said.

Three embarrassed young dolphins swam quickly away to rejoin their pod.

"Are you alright, my blackfish friend?" Argonaut asked.

The elder orca looked at the four humpbacks who had come to his aid. With his thoughts he thanked Argonaut.

The orca said, "I thought, in my long life, I had seen all there was to see. Today, you saved me from the young dolphins. You spoke without sounds. I am humbled and proud to meet the great Inua. Word of your powers has reached my pod. I am in your debt," said the orca.

"We are all special and unique. I did not choose to be an Inua. This role has been chosen for me by a higher spirit. It seems as if I am here to help those in need. No thanks are necessary. I hope you live in peace," Argonaut said.

The old orca swam to Argonaut and touched Argonaut's right pectoral fin with his nose. It was a sign of affection and gratitude. He slowly swam further south towards his pod that lived near the city of Vancouver.

The four humpbacks rejoined their pod. They returned to feeding.

Later than day, T-Rex said to Argonaut, "I am thankful you have shown me the ways of your pod and of the Inua.

I am much happier since I joined you. Mother Biggsy, Little Rex and I will always be by your side."

Argonaut looked at his large friend and smiled.

"I am learning more everyday about being an Inua. I will need you and our pod soon. I see grave danger to me. I am not afraid. I want you here with Raven, Angel, Guardian, Sitka, and the entire pod," Argonaut said.

"You can depend on us to be with you when you are in trouble. All of us would die for our Inua," said T-Rex.

CORONAVIRUS RETURNS

I t was mid-August and tourist season in Telegraph Cove was at its peak. The whale watching ship, Leviathan was at capacity each trip. Cruise ships traveling to and from Alaska were passing frequently through the Vancouver Island straits. Spirit Bear Lodge was fully booked.

Jason received a call from Matt Hawk.

"Jason, I need your help. Both of my parents are ill. They have high fevers and trouble breathing. I have called for a Medivac Helicopter from Nanaimo and it should be here soon. Will you watch the house and Orcella 2 until we return? If I am right, it will be at least two weeks of quarantine for me and much longer for my parents before we all can return to Telegraph Cove," Matt said to his friend.

Jason told Matt, "Of course I will help. Have you cancelled the Orcella 2 tours for the next month?"

"Fortunately, this week we were scheduled to do routine maintenance on the Orcella 2. No tourists are here now. I have contacted all our guests. We cancelled all remaining tours for this year," Matt replied.

"Stay in touch. Let me know as soon as you get a diagnosis. Give Jim and Mary my best," Jason said.

"Thanks buddy. Have to go, helicopter's here," Matt said.

Captain Jim and Mary had recently been to a long-delayed wedding for their niece. After travel restrictions were lifted, Jim and Mary went to Atlanta, Georgia for the wedding. Less than two weeks after their return to Telegraph Cove, they were apparently ill with the resurging COVID-19 virus.

Many experts warned the virus would return, if social distancing, wearing of masks, isolation, and quarantine restrictions were eased. Governments, facing immense pressure from businesses and unemployed workers, removed all work and travel bans by June 1.

As predicted by many experts, the virus was again spreading throughout the world at an alarming pace. There was still no vaccine. Tests for antibodies were unreliable. Apparently, asymptomatic individuals could be carriers of the virus. Reports were surfacing of people, who had previously been infected, becoming ill again.

Premier Guyaen ordered an immediate closure of all Canadian borders. Airports were shuttered. Cruise ships had to harbor at the nearest major port and remain there until further notice. British Columbia government officials halted all passenger traffic on ferries. Only food, medical supplies, and emergency medical workers were allowed on the reduced number of ferries allowed to operate.

The new wave of pandemic infection was difficult for those stuck in Telegraph Cove. There were no large grocery stores. All food had to be imported on regular ferry trips or by trucks from flights landing in Port Hardy.

The situation was also dire on Klemtu. Great Spirit Bear Lodge was packed with guests. Soon there would not be enough food for guest and residents. What made the crisis worse, was First Nation people were genetically more susceptible to the disease. This was proven in the 2020 pandemic, especially among the Navaho tribe members living in the United States.

Chief White Feather called Jason and asked if he had any suggestions on how to get food and supplies to Klemtu. Jason promised to call Commander Mendenhall and ask for aid for his adopted Kitasoo family.

Mendenhall was in Montreal when travel restrictions were enacted. He was able to command his sailors by phone and computer. Mendenhall could not travel back to Vancouver. It was obvious that substantial aid was required for Klemtu, and all other inhabited islands of the area.

Jason emailed Jill White Feather. He wrote "You may be able to get food and other necessary items for Klemtu by seeking help from Project HOPE chapters. If you decide it useful, you may want to contact Bill Gates and ask him to intervene."

Jill responded that she had already reached out to HOPE chapters and Mr. Gates. Help was promised. It would be slow in coming since the Canadian border was closed to all traffic. Ferries had many communities on both sides of the Vancouver straits to supply.

Jason said he would bring whatever supplies he could to help the Kitasoo.

Argonaut had been following events and reached out to Jason.

"My marine animal friends and I can bring fish to Telegraph Cove, Port Hardy, and Klemtu to help feed people," Argonaut said.

Jason worried there could be no rational explanation for this animal behavior. Argonaut's secret had to be protected. Jason and Argonaut developed a plan. Each evening, Argonaut, other humpbacks, orcas, and dolphins would leave fish, crabs, and clams in a large floating wire basket. Jason welded the basket and used a buoyancy collar to keep the basket afloat. Each day, before sunrise, Jason would empty the basket. Jason used his boat, Sadie Princess, to deliver seafood to Klemtu, Telegraph Cove, and islands along the Vancouver straits.

Argonaut asked how Jason was going to explain all the fish and other seafood in his boat. Jason said he would make up a story of buying food from foreign trawlers off the coast of the island.

"Will your friends believe this story?" Argonaut asked.

"They will if a certain large Inua humpback uses his special powers to influence their minds to believe me. Will you help me save the humans?" Jason asked.

"Your people saved my mate and my son. I will help you and your friends. As soon as you make the basket, we will begin filling it with as much food as you need," said Argonaut.

Commander Mendenhall agreed to help Jason and Argonaut. He ordered all Canadian Coast Guard craft to allow Jason's Sadie Princess to operate freely anywhere in Canadian waters without interference. Jason spent all night welding a large metal basket to hold the fish the marine creatures would deliver. He attached a floatation collar. Jason hid the basket in a small harbor away from the main channel of the Johnstone Strait.

Each day at dawn, Jason would empty the basket using a long pole with a wide net. Once fish, crab, and other marine food was onboard Sadie Princess, Jason made deliveries to locations isolated because of the pandemic.

Argonaut stayed close to Jason's boat. His Inua powers enabled Argonaut to convince everyone that seafood was being acquired from offshore fishing boats. There were a lot of people to feed. Jason was working hard to bring food to the Kitasoo, people stranded in Telegraph Cove, and those on other islands.

After a few days, Matt called Jason and said his parents were recovering from the virus. They should be able to leave the hospital within a week. The senior Hawks would stay with Mary's family in Nanaimo.

Jason explained about the food delivery system Argonaut had devised. Matt promised to rent a car in Nanaimo. He would return to Telegraph Cove the following day. Matt would use Orcella 2 to help deliver food to Shearwater, Bella Bella, and Bella Coola. Jason thanked his friend. He said we could use all the help we can get to distribute food the marine life is placing in the basket.

Scientists around the world were working tirelessly to find a vaccine for the Coronavirus. The World Health Organization (WHO) predicted that even with strict social distancing, quarantine procedures, and use of personal protective devices, like masks and gloves, the 2021 version of the pandemic could be much worse than the 2020 mutation of the Coronavirus disease.

Argonaut had foreseen the discovery of a vaccine when the pandemic first appeared in Canada in 2020. He did not know exactly when the cure would be found. He was certain that medicine would be discovered to protect humans.

Jason and Matt worked for six weeks feeding the people of coastal Vancouver Island and western Canada. Kitasoo tribe members trapped small animals. Hunters killed deer, elk, and moose for food.

In late September 2021, a vaccine was discovered by scientists in Geneva, Switzerland. Doses of the medicine was produced in every major country. Vaccinations were given to billions of people.

By December 1, all travel restrictions were lifted. Visitors left Telegraph Cove and Great Spirit Bear Lodge. All travelers were able to return to their homes. The pandemic was over. The vaccine was effective. Life slowly returned to normal.

The humans never knew about all the work done by humpbacks and other marine creatures to help them survive. Jason and Matt thanked Argonaut who shared their appreciation with his pod and all other creatures involved in feeding humans during the crisis.

PROJECT HOPE GETS TWO NEW
VOLUNTEERS

O n September 1, 2021 Commander Wild Bill Mendenhall retired from the Canadian Coast Guard. He had served his country for thirty-five years. He was ready for a different challenge. His first retirement present to himself was to buy a used Bell 206 L-3 helicopter. Wild Bill was certified to fly this type of helicopter. It was an expensive item. However, he would soon find many good uses for his machine.

Project HOPE ran an employment ad on Monster.com. The Kitasoo student directors had taken their small idea and created a worldwide phenomenon. The students wanted a mature, experienced senior administrator to run daily operations of the four-million-member group. The students were so busy issuing newsletters, attending conferences, doing interviews, and writing letters that business matters were not being properly handled. Wild

Bill read the employment ad. He sent his resume to Project HOPE. Susan Standing Bear and Charles Windsong were on the employee search committee. When Mendenhall's resume was received the two directors scheduled an interview with the applicant.

"Commander, congratulations on your retirement. Your resume is incredible. You have all the skills, training, background, and experience we need. We cannot afford to pay you very much," said Susan.

"I am retired, so please call me Bill. I am impressed with your group. I want to help save our planet, too. You six students have done more in two years to help save the earth than anyone I know. I do not need a salary. I have been successful in my investments. I have my Coast Guard retirement income. I will work for one-dollar per year. I will stay in Klemtu two nights per week and live in Port Hardy the rest of the week. We can communicate with Zoom, email, and phone. My helicopter can transport directors to Vancouver or Port Hardy for connecting air travel," said Mendenhall.

Charles asked the former Coast Guard officer if he would be able to take instructions and directions from nineteen-year-old high school graduates.

Mendenhall laughed and said, "You are world renowned celebrities. You have more influence than I ever did as a Coast Guard commander. I have great respect for all of you. I will help Project HOPE, any way I can."

"When can you start?" asked Jill.

"I will arrive by helicopter on Monday and stay here until Wednesday morning. I will fly back to Port Hardy and work remotely from home. Make a list of issues, projects, and topics of concern. I will do everything I can to help your project flourish and continue to grow.

Mendenhall returned to Klemtu the following Monday morning. He met with his young bosses. The new administrator immediately started on their list of issues that required his attention. Structure, organization, and accountability were needed to help the group remain focused and on task.

The retired Coast Guard officer brought decades of experience to Project HOPE. His skills, combined with the energy of the Kitasoo directors, offered an even brighter future for Project HOPE.

When Captain DeFord heard that his former boss was working for Project HOPE, he decided to follow Wild Bill.

Captain DeFord retired two weeks after Wild Bill. Mendenhall discussed hiring Jim DeFord with the six Project HOPE directors. They all agreed that DeFord's knowledge of marine life, water conditions, and the environment of Vancouver straits made him a great addition to HOPE. DeFord agreed to work for the same annual salary as his friend, Bill Mendenhall.

DeFord offered his forty-four-foot converted Nordic Tugboat for use by Project HOPE. Celebrities, major donors, and environmentalists from all over the world wanted to visit Klemtu. DeFord's tugboat was called Hercules. Hercules was built in Burlington, Washington, in the United Sates. DeFord had named his boat after the hero of legends. Interestingly, Hercules had traveled with the mythical Jason, aboard his ship Argos, in the Greek fable of Jason and the Argonauts.

Within a few weeks DeFord and Mendenhall had increased the efficiency of the organization. Both men understood and agreed with directions provided by the Kitasoo directors. Accountability, economies of scale, transparency, improved communication among chapters, and budget control all greatly improved with help from the two former Coast Guard officers.

THREE CALVES GET IN TROUBLE

Little Rex, Rainbow, and the other new humpback calf, Jason, were best friends. They fished and played together each day. The three calves were almost a year old. They were beginning to seek more independence from their parents.

One day in late September, Little Rex asked his friends if they wanted to go on an adventure. Rainbow and Jason both agreed. Soon the three whales quietly swam away from the pod. The three delinquents raced to a place known as orca rubbing beach. The three calves were told by their parents many times to never go to rubbing beach. This place belonged to orcas who might get angry, if calves ventured into the area.

The young humpbacks were disobeying their parents while putting their lives at great risk.

Argonaut knew what the three calves were doing. He had read their minds as they were planning their dangerous adventure. Argonaut asked T-Rex and Raven to follow him, as they quietly swam behind the wayward youngsters. In every species, at one time or another, youngsters want to be independent. What these young humpbacks did not know was that orcas were very protective of their rubbing beach. Orcas can attack and kill a full-grown humpback.

The humpback calves swam up to rubbing beach. They were rolling around on the smooth stones like they had seen orcas do.

Argonaut decided he had to teach these young whales a valuable lesson. Argonaut, using his Inua power, reached out to a nearby pod of transient orcas, currently living in northern Johnstone Strait.

Argonaut said to the orcas, "We have three misbehaving young humpback calves from our pod who are violating your rubbing beach. We want to teach these calves a lesson. They need to learn not to disobey. They should not leave our pod without adult supervision. They must learn to never make orcas angry. Are you willing to help teach them a lesson?"

Four large orcas agreed to help Argonaut with his plan. They swam silently and swiftly to rubbing beach. Orcas surrounded the calves. The large black and white orcas began swimming closer to the unsuspecting humpback calves. With their massive jaws wide open and teeth exposed, the meat-eating giants were almost ready to pounce on the calves.

The calves turned and saw the approaching killer whales and panicked. They could not swim away. They could not fight; they had no teeth. They were outnumbered. They did not have the ability to speak with the approaching orcas. They feared for their lives. The calves all closed their eyes. They each thought this was the end of their lives.

At the very last second, just as the orcas were about to attack, Argonaut called out to the calves and said, "Do you want the orcas to kill you? Did we not tell you to never come here? This is a sacred place to the orcas."

"We're sorry. We meant no harm. We were just playing," said Little Rex.

"You are alive only because these orcas are our friends. We made peace with these mighty fighters after a huge battle before you were born. We help their kind, and they help us. If they were not our friends, you would be dead. Do you understand that you must never leave the protection of our pod? Your pod is your family. We depend on each other. Do not ever violate our trust and disobey," Argonaut told the calves.

We are very sorry all the calves thought to Argonaut. We will never leave the pod without permission again.

Rainbow asked Argonaut, "How can we apologize to the orcas?"

"Each of you will roll over onto your back and expose your underbelly as a sign of deference to the mighty orcas," Argonaut said.

Three calves rolled over and waited for Argonaut to release them from their position of subservience.

"T-Rex, you and Raven take these three misbehaving whales back to the pod while I speak to the orcas," Argonaut said.

The two adults and three calves swam towards Sitka's pod.

Argonaut reached out to the four orcas and said, "Thank you my friends. I believe these youngsters have learned their lesson about running way from our pod. I am thankful for your help. You have kept your promise to be our friends as we have kept ours to help you. This day will become part of the legends passed among generations by our memory keepers. Be safe and thank you again."

Argonaut followed the other humpbacks back to their pod. When he returned, Argonaut called all three calves to him.

"You could have died. Your parents, even the entire pod, would not be able to save you if the orcas had attacked. You were lucky these orcas were our friends and not ones we did not know. As punishment, you will not swim, play, or eat with each other for five sunrises and sunsets. Do you agree with this?" Argonaut asked.

All three calves agreed and they each swam to be with their own mother. Soon, all was forgiven. The lesson of safety in numbers, obeying your elders, and never running away from your family was burned into each calves' memory. From this day forward the calves stayed close to their family. No calves of the Sitka pod ever again violated the space around orca rubbing beach.

HAWAII AGAIN

In late October, Sitka gathered the pod for migration to warmer waters of Hawaii. The whales formed a group around Sitka. They listened to her warnings about boats, nets, and other dangers. Calves would be kept inside a ring of adults to protect them from predators.

Argonaut was asked to lead the pod. He was to use his Inua powers to search out harmful floating debris and incoming boats. Some Japanese fishermen were again violating the international whale hunting agreement, so it was more crucial than ever the pod be alert. Argonaut slept very little on the trip to Hawaii.

None of the whales ate after they left Vancouver waters.

With global warming, their migration stay in Hawaii was being shortened each year. Sitka's pod could return to their home in Johnstone Strait as early as April.

The winter passed quickly. No new calves were born to the pod this year. This was unusual, but not rare in Sitka's life.

The pod now numbered twenty-two whales. Sitka was the oldest of her pod. Rainbow, Little Rex, and Jason were still the three youngest humpbacks.

In late March, the pod began the journey back to Vancouver. Sitka asked Argonaut to swim with her.

Sitka asked Argonaut, "Tell me what it is like to be an Inua."

"It is challenging. I hear so many voices in my thoughts. I feel uncertain of exactly when to listen to which voice. I can see some future events and not others. Sometimes, I am just exhausted by the strain of attempting to save our pod and other creatures in our sanctuary. It is a burden. I am doing the best I can," said Argonaut.

The two whales swam in unison. Breathing, then diving, and returning to surface again.

Sitka said, "I have never known another Inua. You have done many wonderful things for our pod, orcas, humans, and great white sharks. I never realized what a great responsibility you feel for all of us, and our friends. Is there anything we can do to help?"

The Inua thought and said, "Things are as they were meant to be. I can only do so much. You and others in our pod have always been there for me. I have learned much from you. Are there more memories you can share of our past?"

Sitka thought and then told Argonaut the story of the first Inua humpback.

"Memories of the first Inua humpback have been passed down through more seasons than can be counted. It is said that a bright star fell into the water. Heat from the star made the water boiling. A young female humpback swam through the scalding water. As if by magic, she was not harmed. She was changed. She could hear things from vast distances. She saw further into the future than any other of our kind. She swam faster than before. She dove deeper. She grew more powerful each day. Legend says she could stop a predator with her thoughts. She saved seals, dolphins, and sea lions from sharks and orcas. She was able to help her pod find food. She had many children with her mate," Sitka explained.

"What was the name of this ancient Inua?" Argonaut

asked.

"She was called Blakkur. She had an all-black tail with just one small dot. It is very rare for a whale to have a tail with that coloring," Sitka said.

Argonaut and Sitka continued to swim. Argonaut asked if he might be a descendant of Blakkur. Sitka smiled and nodded her head.

"All whale Inua are from the blood line of ancient Blakkur. There are many whales all over the earth. There may be other Inua humpbacks," said Sitka.

After one final day of swimming across the vast Pacific Ocean, the pod returned to the straits near Vancouver.

Argonaut sensed a new threat to he and his family. He tried to clear his mind but a clear vision never formed.

Angel asked her mate what was troubling him.

Argonaut explained his feeling of fear for the near future.

"Is it more hunters like when I was taken?" asked Angel.

"No. This is a threat from humans but different then when you were stolen from us. I know we will not be taken. We are in danger. I will try to understand more," Argonaut told Angel.

ARGONAUT'S SECRET

Brigitte Fisher was the most renowned and respected broadcast journalist in Canada. She anchored a one-hour weekly television show called "Epic News". The program was shown on Sunday evenings at eight. Ms. Fisher had received seven Gemini awards, Canadian equivalent of the Emmy awards in the United States. Her forte was in-depth reporting on scientific, cultural, and economic events of Canadian regional and national importance.

Her documentary on cartels importing illicit drugs into Canada was the highest viewed news broadcast in Canadian history. Stories about financial scandals, environmental disasters, political wrong doings, and more had made Fisher a household name.

Fisher did approximately twenty news shows a year. Her broadcasts were made from different locations in various provinces. Her home was near Stanley Park, not far from Vancouver harbor. Many of her investigative reports took weeks or months to produce. She had a large number of runners in every province. A runner is an entry level person trying to break into the broadcasting industry. These runners searched out tips and leads for stories that might intrigue Fisher. A runner who found a story of interest to Fisher, might be promoted to an assistant on her staff. A very successful runner eventually might reach reporter status.

In June 2022, three different runners filed memos with Fisher. Each memo mentioned unusual events reportedly occurring near the northern end of Vancouver Island. One memo would have not produced much interest. Three memos, involving different incidents in waters of northern Vancouver Island, meant something.

Anne Taylor was the first runner to contact Ms. Fisher. Taylor wrote in an email about reports of a significant confrontation between humpbacks and orcas in waters of the harbor near Telegraph Cove. Multiple witnesses had photographed and videoed the event. What made such a conflict remarkable was united battle lines formed by humpbacks. There is no known precedent for this type of behavior among humpbacks. According to spectators, over fifty humpbacks had fought side-by-side to defeat an orca attack on humpback calves.

By itself, this event was interesting. It was not news-worthy enough to warrant investigation by Ms. Fisher.

Several weeks after the Taylor report, Fisher received a second whale related communication. Jessie Elliott wrote to Ms. Fisher about the sinking of a sailboat. Again, this is not an extraordinary event. Boating accidents are relatively common. Several people camping on an island near the crash site swore that orcas had used ropes to help people safely to shore. This was more than unusual. Behavior like this by orcas had never been reported. If orcas seen helping humans were transients, then it was even more remarkable. Transients were meat eaters. It was difficult to believe orcas would help and not attack humans. Ms. Elliott had sworn statements from several witnesses to rescue of humans by orcas. There were now reports of two incredible events occurring in the same general area. Ms. Fisher sensed a potential block-buster story in the making.

These two events in combination piqued Ms. Fisher's interest enough that she considered an investigative trip to northern Vancouver Island.

What finally convinced Fisher to start researching the incidents was a report from Janet Coggan. Ms. Coggan had a sworn and notarized statement from Preston Blake, an island-hopping pilot living in Port Hardy. While flying tourists to Haida Gwaii, Blake saw a large group of orcas and humpbacks confront several great white sharks near the northern entrance to Johnstone Strait. There was no violence. After circling the marine animals for as long as possible, Blake returned to Port Hardy before his plane ran out of fuel. He had clear pictures of the whale and shark encounter on his phone.

Fisher knew there were some remarkable events occurring in waters of the straits of Vancouver. She did not know how these three runner filings were related, but she was certain they were connected. Fisher became famous by following her instincts. She did not believe in coincidence. The challenge for Fisher was to discover the truth about three different incidents reported by her runners.

Fisher decided to go undercover to investigate these three whale related reports. She disguised herself with colored contact lenses, a wig, and lifts in her shoes. She looked different than her broadcast image. She used a false identity. Fisher began her research in the city Victoria on Vancouver Island.

She learned of the capture of a North Korean ship that had kidnapped a whale from the Johnstone Strait. She talked to Coast Guard crewman. Fisher heard rumors that Panamanian pirates aboard a North Korean ship were caught trying to steal a "magic whale." Fisher was now certain there was an incredible story here.

Fisher's next stop was in Nanaimo. The reporter talked to British Columbia Ferry workers who confirmed the rumor that orcas had helped survivors of a wreck swim to shore. These ferry workers had not witnessed the event, but it was widely accepted as true by ferry staff.

By chance, Fisher learned the best tour operators in the northern part of Vancouver straits were the Hawks. She called the Hawk tour company. Fisher, due to a last-minute cancellation, was able to get a spot on the next trip aboard Orcella 2. A traveler from Brazil had to cancel their trip. There was available space. Fisher registered for the trip using her fake identity. She traveled under the name April Calfee.

At the same time Fisher, under her false name, was traveling from Nanaimo to Telegraph Cove, Argonaut asked Jason to meet him near Biggs Island. Argonaut also asked Matt Hawk to join them at dawn the next day.

Jason and Matt arrived aboard Sadie Princess. They put on their wet suits and scuba gear. They dove to meet Argonaut. The Inua was clearly disturbed and highly agitated. He spoke to his friends as soon as they were close.

"There is a new danger to me, Angel, and my entire pod. Someone is aware of my special powers. The person is trying to discover which whale in our sanctuary is special. She is arriving tomorrow to stay with the Hawk family. She is booked for the next trip aboard Orcella 2. She will search for truth about my Inua powers. If she learns of my Inua abilities, then my life will be ruined. I, my family, and likely our entire pod will have to flee. We would need to leave our pod and our home. We would have to hide far from our sanctuary. I am very worried," Argonaut said.

Matt asked Argonaut how he knew these things to be true. Argonaut and Jason both looked at Matt and shook their heads.

Matt said using his thoughts, "Right. Silly question. Argonaut knows."

Argonaut translated Matt's thoughts for Jason.

Jason asked if Argonaut knew the name of the person who was trying to learn their secret. Argonaut told his friends the reporters real name is Brigitte Fisher, but she is using the name April Calfee.

Matt explained that Fisher had just filled an open tour spot. He asked if it was a good idea to cancel her registration.

Argonaut said, "If we seem anxious or afraid, we will confirm her suspicions. I sense she is a very smart person. She will not be easily deceived. She knows of the sailboat crash, the orca attack, the kidnapping of Angel, and the confrontation with the great whites. She is determined and very dangerous."

"Does she know which whale is responsible for the incidents that have occurred?" Jason asked Argonaut.

"So far, I am not specifically identified. My entire pod is suspected as being involved. I may be putting our pod at risk, if this woman discovers the truth. We need to keep her from learning my secret or convince her to keep the truth from becoming public knowledge," Argonaut said.

"I know Ms. Fisher's reputation. She is ruthless. She is a very successful reporter. She will not stop looking until she uncovers the truth," Jason said.

Matt suggested that Jason join the tour aboard Orcella 2 to help discover what Ms. Fisher knew about Argonaut and his powers. Jason agreed. He met the tour, at the docked Orcella 2, in Telegraph Cove harbor the following morning.

After introductions and usual safety lecture, Orcella 2 left Telegraph Cove for the marine sanctuary. Orcella 2 was soon motoring among a huge pod of dolphins. Photographers were snapping pictures. A large pod of orcas swam by Orcella 2 heading north. The water was calm, the sky was a brilliant blue, there were no clouds, and just a light breeze. Guests aboard Orcella 2 were enjoying themselves.

Fisher joined Captain Hawk on the bridge. They talked of his long career as a Canadian Coast Guard officer. Fisher asked about Orcella 2. Captain Jim was happy to discuss his boat and career.

When the reporter quizzed Captain Hawk about magic whales, he laughed.

"Ms. Calfee, every creature in this sanctuary is magical. I have spent most of my life on boats and ships. Very little about these creatures surprises me. Their migration, singing, attention to their young, and ability to act in unison to catch food is magical," Captain Jim explained.

Ms. Fisher was not easily deterred or distracted.

"I have heard rumors that whales in these waters have saved humans. Reports have surfaced of whales and orcas fighting with each other and then making peace. Supposedly, a large gathering of orcas and humpbacks fought off a group of great whites trying to enter the Johnstone Strait. Do you have any comment on these reports?" asked Fisher.

Captain Jim knew April Calfee was Brigitte Fisher.

Captain Jim turned to Fisher and said, "Sometimes what we hear from others is not exact. I remember a game we played as children. One person told another a secret. By the time it was retold several times the secret bore no resemblance to the actual story. You remind me of someone famous. Have I seen you on television?"

Fisher said, "Many people mistake me for someone else."

"There you go. People make mistakes. Stories get exaggerated. It's like in ancient times, when sailors mistook manatees for mermaids. Sailors thought they were right, but they were not," said wise old Captain Jim.

Fisher then tried to get answers from Matt.

"No, I have never seen a magic whale. There are myths and legends among the First Nation tribes of western Canada. I have heard the same stories in the maritime provinces, Australia, and Hawaii. Perhaps someone has confused myth with fact," Matt said.

Brigitte Fisher was no fool. She realized that neither of the Hawks was going to divulge any information regarding rumors.

On the second day of the tour, Fisher asked the same questions of Jason Belliveau. He repeated the same answers.

"I know of no magic whales. There have been stories of animals saving humans for as long as man has sailed the seas. Life here has been quiet and calm for centuries. There is nothing special about these straits except the beauty of the area and the animals that live here," Jason said.

Ms. Fisher told the Hawks that she had a chance to visit Klemtu the following day. She wanted a chance to see a Spirit Bear. She hired Wild Bill Mendenhall to fly her from Telegraph Cove to Klemtu. While riding in the helicopter, Fisher asked Mendenhall if he had witnessed any unusual or exceptional behavior among the whales of Vancouver Island. Jason had called Mendenhall to explain the real identity of his passenger.

Mendenhall thought for a few moments before he answered.

"I have seen an adult humpback leap one-hundred times in less than two hours. I have witnessed humpbacks migrate almost three-thousand miles to Hawaii and return to this sanctuary without use of a map. I have heard the mystical calls of humpbacks from over twenty-miles away. I have listened to the echo location clicks of orcas and dolphins. I have watched a school of over one-thousand dolphins swim and play for hours then vanish into the depths. These are real facts. These are remarkable behaviors. It is what these creatures do and have done since time began," said Wild Bill.

Soon they arrived at Klemtu. April Calfee (really Brigitte Fisher) paid for her flight and thanked Mendenhall. The reporter, using her false identity, was met by Chief White Feather. After the two introduced themselves to each other, Fisher was shown to her room in Great Spirit Bear Lodge.

Fisher spent two days with a First Nation guide hiking the forests near Klemtu. She was fortunate to see a Spirit Bear. The jaded, hardened, reporter was moved by her time with the Spirit Bear. The longer she spent in the area around Vancouver Island the more connected she felt to the area and its wildlife.

It is said by many, seeing a Spirit Bear is a life altering experience. There is a religious like awakening when the rare and wonderful bear is seen in the wild.

Fisher had time to speak with the six Project HOPE directors while on Klemtu. Project HOPE continued to grow. Its impact was spreading. Jill White Feather gave Ms. Fisher a tour of HOPE's headquarters. An old tourist cabin had been refurbished for use as HOPE's central office. Wild Bill Mendenhall had assisted the group in upgrading their computers. More wi-fi links had been installed. A small recording studio had been built.

After her stay at Great Spirit Bear Lodge, Ms. Fisher started the return trip to Port Hardy aboard Sadie Princess. Jason Belliveau had offered to transport Ms. Fisher to the airport. As they were crossing Johnstone Strait, Fisher again asked Jason about magic whales.

"I have heard stories of fantastic encounters between humpbacks and orcas. Great whites were held off by a large group of whales and orcas. Supposedly humans were saved by orcas after a ship wreck. Can you share any information about these stories?" she asked.

Jason replied, "What do you think of this part of Canada? Are you impressed by the beauty and majesty of the animals and environment? If the things you mention are true and the information became known, what would happen?"

"Do you know who I am?" asked the reporter.

Jason laughed, "Everyone knows who you are. You have one of the most famous faces in all of Canada. We did not reveal your secret because we respected your privacy. Tell me, do you respect the marine life of these waters?"

"If there are intelligent maritime creatures living here, humans should know of them," said the reporter.

"I know for certain that if there is even a suggestion that whales, orcas, dolphins, or any other marine life have previously undiscovered abilities, this sanctuary would be destroyed. Tourists, hunters, zoos, and aquariums would be in every bay and harbor. Pollution would increase dramatically. Animals that live here would never have peace. Habitats would be destroyed. Migration and hibernation patterns would be altered. Once done, damage could never be undone. Is this what you want to see?" Jason asked.

"I report the facts. People have a right to know. Secrets help no one. Maybe there are things we can learn from the animals. If I tell the story, tourism will increase dramatically. More people will move to the area. Incomes will rise," she said.

With disdain, Jason spoke to the reporter and said, "This land and its waters have been pristine since the beginning of time. Project HOPE directors you met are devoting all their time and energy trying to make changes to help stop pollution and climate change. Destroying this incredible area by writing a story is not worth it."

"Are you confirming the rumors that there are special whales and other creatures living here?" she asked.

Jason reached out to Argonaut. He asked if the Inua had been following his conversation with the reporter. Argonaut replied that indeed, he had been listening to Jason and Fisher.

"I want to meet this lady. I will try and reason with her," Argonaut said.

"That is a very bad idea. She will destroy you, your pod, and our home. We must keep your Inua powers a secret. Disclosing your voice to this reporter will be the beginning of the end for you," Jason spoke to Argonaut using his thoughts.

"It is a risk I have to take. She will not stop looking for answers unless I can convince her to stop. Slow down. Let me catch you. I will be there as quickly as I can," Argonaut told Jason.

Jason slowed Sadie Princess to an idle and waited for Argonaut to appear. Once Argonaut reached the bow of the boat he slowly rose to the surface and spyhopped. Fisher was freighted by the massive creature.

"Ms. Fisher, I am the Inua Argonaut. I have come to talk with you. I am here to ask your help in keeping me and my pod safe," Argonaut said.

"I knew it. My instincts are never wrong. You are a magical whale. I was born to report this story. I will be the most famous journalist of all time," she said.

"What price will we pay for your fame? My mate, my son, and my grandchild will certainly be killed or captured. We will be studied, dissected, and soon become extinct. Humpbacks, orcas, and dolphins have lived here for more seasons than man can count. With one story you can end our existence. You have seen the beauty of our home. You have met the wonderful people that live and work here. The Kitasoo tribe is one with the land, as it is now. You have seen the Spirit Bear. If you speak, all will be lost," said Argonaut.

"Do you really expect me to keep quiet about a telepathic whale?" she asked.

"I hope you will consider what damage you will do, if you reveal my secret. I have done only good things with my powers. I have helped save people. I have helped many creatures. I have made peace between natural enemies. If you strip me of my powers, by exposing me to humans, then you will ruin any hope of my doing more good things for the world," Argonaut told Fisher.

Fisher was quiet for several minutes. She looked at the Inua. She thought to herself that perhaps she could negotiate a compromise.

"I have spent my whole life wanting to tell stories. I understand your concerns. I do agree the risk of destruction is great, if I disclose facts of your Inua skill. Would you be willing to tell me about your adventures if I do not disclose the source? I will write a fiction novel. It will be set on another planet. No mention of you, Jason, or any other creature from your home, will be included in my story. If you promise to let me know of your Inua deeds, I will promise to keep your secret safe. Do we have a deal?" she asked.

Argonaut told Jason about his conversation with the reporter. He asked Jason if he trusted her. Jason was worried. If the reporter left the area with knowledge of Argonaut, she might be tempted to write about his powers.

"My Inua friend, I do not know if we can trust this woman. The fame and accolades she would earn by disclosing your talents may be too tempting for her," Jason said.

Argonaut listened to his friend. He made one of the most important decisions of his life.

He again spyhopped by Sadie Princess and looked Fisher directly in the eyes.

"I have decided to trust you. You should know that my powers include seeing into the future. If you violate my trust, I have the ability to clear your memory of all you have learned. I can reach you wherever you are. I will watch, listen, and if you are truthful, I will share future stories of my Inua powers. Set your book on a different world. Maybe if people read about animals doing good things, it will help us. We have a deal," said Argonaut.

Jason docked Sadie Princess at Port Hardy. Ms. Fisher left on a 4:30 afternoon flight to Vancouver. While in flight home, Fisher reached out to Argonaut.

"You can read my mind, can't you?" she asked Argonaut.

"Yes. I never am totally asleep. I trust you, but if you break your promise my Inua power will reach you. All you have learned will be lost from your memory. I have never acted in anger. But know this, I will defend my pod and my sanctuary with my life," Argonaut said.

"I understand. I have never divulged a source. I am going to take time away from my job as a reporter to work on my first fiction novel. I have already decided on a title. My book will be titled CETACEA – WHERE WHALES ARE RULERS," said Fisher.

Ms. Fisher's book became an international bestseller. She permanently left her job as a reporter. She often visited Johnstone Strait and Klemtu. She and Argonaut became friends. As promised, he continued to share his adventures with her.

ARGONAUT'S FAMILY

Raven and his father were swimming near Quadro Island searching for krill.

"Father, you have never spoken of your mother and father. What happened to them?" Raven asked.

Argonaut was very still. He looked at his son. He knew this day would sometime come. He was not sure he was ready to tell his story. He had to be truthful with his son.

"Raven, you know the story of my birth and the lightning strike. My father's name was Knolhval. It is an ancient name from a distant land where whales like us first lived. My mother's name was Bella. I was her second calf. My older sister was named Flickr. My sister was two winters old when I was born. We made the migration to our sanctuary. We were safe and happy. It

213

was an uneventful spring and summer. Next fall we returned to our winter home.

During my second migration tragedy struck. Your grandmother, Bella, was feeding. She suddenly became violently ill. She died within a short time. There was nothing we could do to save her. We did not know why she died.

After my mother's death, my father became quiet and distant. Nothing seemed to make him enjoy life.

During the next migration, Flickr was trapped in a floating net. We tried to keep her afloat, eventually she died. Knolhval became wild with anger and despair. Spirit, who was the matriarch before Sitka, tried to console him. He would not listen. We made it to our winter home. My father was never near the pod. He would not swim with us. He was so lonely and sad. My heart broke for him.

We made our return migration to our island sanctuary. My father was losing weight. He would not sing or speak to anyone. At that time, I did not have my Inua powers. I was no comfort in his time of suffering.

Knolhval made the quest to our ancient humpback burial grounds with me. He spoke very little. Like you, I completed the quest. My father and I returned to our pod.

The night of our return from our quest, my father left. He swam away late at night, without saying goodbye. The sky was dark. Waves were large. Wind was loud. None of us knew he was gone, until the next morning.

We called out. He did not answer. We swam from Port Hardy to Vancouver. He could not be found. I lost my mother, my sister, and my father. I was an orphan. I had our pod, but I was sad, alone, and scared," Argonaut told his son.

Raven felt sorry for his father. He swam next to Argonaut. He rubbed his pectoral fin on his father. Argonaut was moved by his son's affection.

"Father, now that your Inua powers are so great could you find Knolhval?" Raven asked.

Argonaut told his son, "I sometimes feel his presence, in the cold waters far to the north of us. He is alone, sad, and has no pod."

"Can you reach out to him? Are you willing to invite him home, to be with us?" asked Raven.

"As great as my powers may be, I know if my father wishes to be sad and alone that is his choice," Argonaut said.

"Knolhval does not know you have a mate, a son, and a grandson. Maybe if you reached out to him and asked him to visit us, he might return and choose to stay here. It would do no harm. Don't you want to see your father?" Raven asked.

"I miss my father. He was a kind and caring parent before my mother and sister died. I think a large part of him died when they were taken from us. Maybe it is time to reach out and touch his mind. I will try. Thank you, my son, for talking to me. I needed you to help me make this decision," Argonaut said.

Often, parents can learn from their offspring just as young creatures learn from their elders.

As Argonaut and Raven swam north to rejoin the pod, the Inua quieted his mind and focused. Argonaut tried finding his father in the cold waters far to the north. Inua thoughts raced across vast distances until Knolhval was found.

"Father, it is I, your son, Argonaut. I have missed you for more than five winters. I have a son, a mate, and a grandson. You are a great grandfather. Your pod misses you. We want to be with you. We have much to talk about. I can feel your pain and sadness. If you return home, we can share our lives with you. Maybe with our help, you can learn to be like you were in the past. I know you can never replace Bella and Flickr. We are family to you. Please, consider my wish. If you want to return, I can meet you near Port Hardy. We can talk, father to son. I want my son, Raven, to know his grandfather. If you hear my thoughts, you know that I am Inua. I have many stories to tell you. Please father, come home," Argonaut thought to his father.

Six sunrises later Argonaut heard his father in his mind.

"Son, I am at the entrance to the harbor near Port Hardy. I would like to see you. I have heard of a famous Inua who can talk to other creatures using his mind. I did not know that you, my son, were the famous Inua," Knolhval said.

"Yes, father. I am the humpback Inua. I am your son. I am Bella's son. I will be by your side as quickly as I can. Wait for me, please," Argonaut spoke.

Within two hours, Argonaut reached Port Hardy. He sensed his father's presence. Neither whale spoke or thought. They stared at each other. Argonaut was much bigger than when his father saw him last. Knolhval had lost weight.

Finally, Argonaut asked his father, "How are you?"

His father answered, "For many years I have been alone, sad, and away from my family. When I lost your mother and sister I could not eat. I could not think clearly. I fell into a great black hole of despair. My anger and frustration overwhelmed me. I thought only of my own pain. I could not bear the thought I might lose you as well, so I ran away. I hid in the darkest waters. I am ashamed that I left you. I did not have the courage to face you, or to even say goodbye."

"Father, evil men took my mate for just a few hours. I thought she was lost. I almost used my Inua power to kill the evil ones who took her. If Angel or Raven were killed, I'd be lost. I think I understand something of your suffering. Will you come home with me and meet your grandson and his son?" Argonaut said.

Knolhval nodded. Together, for the first time in many years, Argonaut and his father swam side by side.

KNOLHVAL MEETS THE POD

Argonaut and his father swam south towards the waiting pod. All the mature humpbacks knew Knolhval. The youngest of the pod had never heard his name, until today.

Sitka gathered the pod in Alert Bay. Soon Knolhval and his son swam into view. Sitka was first to swim to her long absent friend. She touched noses with Knolhval.

"Welcome home. You have been away from us for too long. We have missed you," Sitka said.

Next in line to greet the new arrival was T-Rex. The two old friends touched pectoral fins. No words were necessary. T-Rex was glad to see Knolhval. Of all the whales, T-Rex best understood the sadness of being alone and how a whale could be happier with a pod.

Argonaut next introduced Angel. She bowed before her mate's father.

"Welcome home, father. Argonaut has missed you very much. We are happy you have come to live with us. Our family is proud to be with you," Angel said.

Angel introduced her son, Raven, and his mate, Biggsy. Both young whales bowed before Knolhval. They both said how were happy to meet him.

Raven introduced calves Jason, Rainbow, and Little Rex.

Knolhval looked in awe at the expanded number of humpies in Sitka's pod.

"You have all done well to have so many healthy young whales in the pod. I have heard stories of a magical whale who made peace with the orcas; made peace with the great whites; saved his son from drowning in a net and much more. I am anxious to hear more about the Inua Argonaut and his adventures," Knolhval told the group.

It was getting late in the day and Sitka set the watch for the night. The whales swam to the far side of Cortes Island to rest.

"I have been gone for so long. Much has changed, yet the land and water seem the same," Knolhval said to Argonaut.

"I have much to tell you and questions I want to ask. I can speak to all creatures using my Inua powers. I can read minds. I am able to feel what others feel. I can see some of the future. I am Inua, but without you here, I felt incomplete," Argonaut told his father.

Knolhval looked at Argonaut and said, "Why did you ask me to return? I abandoned you when you were young. Did you not hate me for leaving?"

"You are my father. My love for you is not bound by time or distance. You did what you had to do to survive many horrors of your life. My place is not to judge you. As your son, I honor you. You gave me life. You took me on a quest to see the ancient burial site. We are together again. There is much you can teach Raven, Jason, Little Rex, and others in our pod. We will go slowly interacting with the pod. This will allow you to adjust being here, among your family and friends. It is hard to be alone for so long, then be surrounded by so many other whales. If I can help, just think of your need and I will hear you," said Argonaut.

"Tell me what it is like being Inua. Do you enjoy your

power and responsibility?" father asked his son.

"I had no choice. I realized one day that I could do more things than other whales. I try to be good, kind, fair, and brave. Other creatures respect me, but not because I am powerful. Others seem to understand that I want to help. I try to be as brave and kind as I can. With the assistance of Raven, T-Rex, Guardian, and my human friends Jason, Matt and Captain Jim I have done many things of which I am proud. It is hard to listen to the thoughts of so many others. I am only one whale. Being an Inua is demanding and tiring, but it is who I am. I will always do my best," said Argonaut.

Argonaut reached out to Jason and told him that Knolhval, his father, had returned. He invited Jason and Matt to meet his long absent father at dawn by Telegraph Cove Harbor.

Jason told Argonaut that he and Matt would be there at dawn.

Aboard Orcella 2, Matt and Jason left the harbor at dawn. They soon were met by father and son humpbacks. Jason and Matt put on their dry suits and scuba gear. They joined the whales in the calm waters of the harbor. Argonaut explained to Knolhval how he had met Jason and began conversing, using a talking machine.

Once Argonaut understood his Inua power, he could talk to Jason and other humans without the machine.

Knolhval was stunned as he listened to his son. He touched his nose to the hands of first Jason then Matt. He told Argonaut to greet his friends and tell them he was also their friend.

Argonaut beamed with pride as his father was meeting his human friends. Argonaut was seeing more of the future and was certain his father and these two humans were going to be part of a major event in his life.

Time passes slowly in the Johnstone Strait. Knolhval played with the calves. He ate and gained back his strength. He took his turn on night watch. He met orcas that had made peace with humpbacks. He was very glad to be back with his pod. He never again wanted to be alone in the dark and cold Artic waters.

WHO LIVES AND WHO DIES?

Argonaut felt happier now than at any other time in his life. His father was with the pod. His mate, son, and grandson were healthy. Disease that had affected the humans had passed. There was plenty of food. Peace was still in effect with orcas and great whites.

Jason visited the pod as often as he could. Captain Jim and Matt often saw the pod while touring with guests on Orcella 2. It had been a warm spring. Summer felt several degrees warmer than usual.

Argonaut knew Project HOPE was working to stop the warming of his sanctuary waters. Much work remained before global temperature change could be stopped.

In late May, a large transient orca entered Vancouver harbor. He was not one of the orcas that had made peace with Argonaut. This was a very dangerous killer whale. In March 2011, this orca and his pod were swimming in Japanese waters near the Fukushima Nuclear Power Plant when a horrible accident occurred. An earthquake triggered a tsunami near the Fukushima reactors. The earthquake caused the reactors to shut down. A series of system failures allowed vast quantities of contaminated water to flow into the Pacific Ocean. The flow of contaminated water continued for several years. The World Health Organization (WHO) predicted that human health would not be affected. It may take up to forty years to clean up the affected area.

Effects of contamination on fish and other marine life, from the disaster, are not known. Some suggest quick decay of iodine 131, a large portion of the effluent from the reactors, may reduce damage to marine life. Truth is, no one knows the extent of damage to sea creatures from the nuclear accident.

A large pod of transient orcas lived near the site of the nuclear accident. They ate fish that were contaminated. They breathed air that carried radioactive material. Fukushima orcas had the highest concentration of nuclear poisoning of any species. Within four years, orcas started dying from nuclear poisoning. What had once been a pod of nineteen orcas had been reduced to one now entering straits near Vancouver Island.

The killer whale swimming north from Vancouver Harbor was in terrible pain. His brain and other internal organs were severely damaged by nuclear poisoning.

Most of his teeth had fallen out. His skin was molting. He was weakening quickly. He still was dangerous.

He was like a rabid animal. He was not acting in a rational way. He wanted to kill whatever he could. Pain he felt was beyond his capacity to bear.

Knolhval, Raven, and T-Rex were playing with the young calves near Comax. Argonaut and the remaining humpbacks were feeding on a large bait ball several miles north.

Southern resident orcas, who were friends with the Sitka pod, saw the sick transient orca swim north towards the unsuspecting humpbacks. The southern orcas reached out to Argonaut with their thoughts. Orcas warned Argonaut of the dangerous transient approaching from the south.

Argonaut felt the approach of the killer whale. He was too far away to intervene directly, if there was an attack.

Argonaut used his Inua power to reach his father, son, and T-Rex.

"There is a large killer whale swimming toward you from Vancouver Harbor. He is close. I cannot reach his thoughts. The orca is sick and very dangerous. He wants to hurt every creature he can. I cannot get to you in time to stop him. I will try reaching into his mind, but there is so much pain that he may not react to my thoughts. I might not be able to stop him. You are in great danger," Argonaut said.

Knolhval told Raven to get on his right side. T-Rex took up his position to the left of Knolhval. The three calves swam behind the larger mature whales.

Argonaut was swimming as fast as he could to reach his family and friends. The orca's mind was unlike any Argonaut had touched before. Anger and pain had caused the whale to lose the ability to understand Argonaut.

The orca saw three whales. He went straight for them with his jaws wide open. At the last second, Raven and T-Rex each struck the orca with one of their fifteen-foot pectoral fins. The orca was stunned. Knolhval dove quickly. He breached under the stunned orca. The killer whale was thrown five feet into the air.

T-Rex breached directly onto the hurt orca. Raven used his fluke to repeatedly strike the sick killer whale.

Argonaut finally reached his family and friends. He ordered them to stop attacking the dying orca.

"No. This orca attacked us. He could have killed us and the calves. He must be killed or he will attack again. We were lucky to stun him," said T-Rex.

"I forbid any further attacks on this orca. This is a sick and dying creature. He lived near our winter home when his pod was poisoned. I feel his pain. He is very near death. Please, let's give him dignity in a quiet end of his life, free of pain and violence," Argonaut asked.

Raven, T-Rex, and the three calves slowly started swimming back to the pod. Knolhval stayed with his son as they faced the dying orca.

"What can you do to ease his pain?" Knolhval asked.

"I will try and reach into his memory. He may be able to recall his family. I will try to calm him. Will you stay with me?" Argonaut asked his father.

"I promise to never leave you again," said Knolhval.

Argonaut swam closer to the orca and reached deep into his mind. He helped the orca remember a time before the illness. The orca became calmer. He knew he was dying.

"Will you take me to a place I have heard is near here?" asked the orca.

"We will do all we can to ease your passing. Where do you want to go?" Argonaut asked.

"Rubbing beach. I want to feel the cool smooth stones on my burning skin. I will die in peace, if you can help me," said the orca.

Argonaut explained the request to his father. They took turns carrying the orca on their backs. It was hard work but rubbing beach was close. When the orca was placed on the stones, he closed his eyes. He remembered his family.

"Thank you, Inua. I'm sorry I tried to hurt your family. I was so sick I did not know what I was doing. I will pass in peace to the great beyond, where my family waits for me," said the orca as he quietly died.

Argonaut called his friends, the southern resident orcas, to thank them for the warning of the sick transient. He explained what had happened. The sick orca died in peace at rubbing beach.

The killer whales told Argonaut they would be at rubbing beach in a few minutes. They would take the dead orca far into the ocean and say goodbye, as orcas do.

Knolhval turned to his son and said, "I am beginning to understand what it means to be an Inua. I am proud to be your father. We would have killed the orca if you had not stopped us. You used your kind and gentle heart to make his last moments peaceful. You truly are a great and wise Inua."

"I would have killed the orca to save you and the others. My hope was to reach deep into his mind and find some memory he could enjoy before he died. We did a good thing today father. Let's rejoin our family," said Argonaut.

MAYDAY, MAYDAY

After Wild Bill Mendenhall retired, Lieutenant Commander Peggy Pierstorff was promoted to commanding officer of all western Canadian Coast Guard operations. After her promotion, the commander was making visits to various ships and ports under her command.

Today, she was in Port Hardy inspecting the newest addition to the Coast Guard helicopter fleet. The Skiorsky MH-60T Jayhawk is a twin-engine medium-range helicopter. The Canadian Coast Guard was often called on to rescue ships at sea.

As Commander Pierstorff was touring the Jayhawk, a distress call was broadcast over base radio.

"Mayday, Mayday, this is Pacifica Airlines flight 989 from Anchorage to Port Hardy. We are located twenty-one miles northwest of Port Hardy, British Columbia. We suffered total engine shutdown. There are seven passengers and two crew members aboard. Estimate hitting the ocean in less than sixty seconds. Will deploy life rafts and issue life vests. Need immediate help. Do you copy? Over." said the pilot.

The coast guard radio operator at Port Hardy responded, "Flight 989, received your message. We have you on our radar. A rescue helicopter will be at your location within ten minutes. Do you have emergency beacons aboard your life craft? Over."

"Affirmative. We will deploy flares and activate emergency beacons. We are approaching water now. Last transmission," said the pilot.

Port Hardy base commander ordered the MH-60T Jayhawk airborne with instructions to locate and rescue all survivors. Captain Bruce Brient was the chief pilot of the Jayhawk. He and his crew were ready to depart Port Hardy within three minutes of receiving the distress call. Commander Pierstorff joined the rescue flight to observe her crew in action.

Passengers on the Pacifica flight included Wild Bill Mendenhall and all six Kitasoo Project HOPE directors. The group was returning from an International Symposium in Anchorage, Alaska on global warming.

Mendenhall made the trip as chaperone and administrative aid to the six Project HOPE directors.

As soon as the plane hit water, the pilot opened the main cabin door. She threw two life rafts into the Pacific Ocean. Each passenger was wearing their life vest. Four Kitasoo jumped from the plane into the first raft. The last two Kitasoo, Mendenhall, pilot, and co-pilot all boarded the second raft. The plane was still afloat. The emergency beacons on both life rafts were activated. The water was calm, wind was light. It was early afternoon. Within ten minutes the Canadian Coast Guard helicopter was on site. Two rescue divers jumped into the water near the rafts.

After determining all survivors were in good condition, the helicopter lowered a basket. Rescuers began bringing one survivor at a time aboard the aircraft. It took almost an hour for all nine victims of the crash to be brought aboard the helicopter.

Once everyone was secured, the helicopter turned towards Port Hardy. As soon as they were on the ground, Mendenhall called Chief White Feather and informed him of the place crash. He assured the Chief that all First Nation young people were safe. Jim DeFord and his tug, Hercules, were at Port Hardy. DeFord offered to take the Hope directors home to Klemtu.

Soon all Project HOPE directors were safely on their way home. Mendenhall and Pierstorff interviewed the pilot and co-pilot about the near tragedy. Pilot, Captain Julie Sculley, was a veteran of thirty years commercial flying. Until today, she had a perfect safety record. Co-pilot, Max Upman, had more than ten years' service with Pacifica.

The plane involved was a recently remodeled 2009 Piper Jetprop. The engine had less than fifty hours since it's last overhaul. Both pilot and co-pilot had done a manual safety inspection. As required by airline rules, pilots had used pre-flight checklists before takeoff.

The accident was reported to the Canadian Traffic Safety Board (TSB). Investigators would be at Port Hardy the following morning to interview the crew. Maintenance records would be checked.

Captain Sculley explained to Mendenhall and Pierstorff, "We experienced sudden total engine failure. All gauges read normal until the incident. I tried switching from starboard to port fuel tanks. The engines would not restart. I know the aircraft like the back of my hand. What happened should not have happened. There should have been a warning of some kind.

The USS Independence was steaming from Seattle to Dutch Harbor, Alaska on her next rotation. Captain Steve Waters heard the rescue calls from the Pacifica plane to Port Hardy over ship's radio. He called Port Hardy Coast Guard station. Waters reported he had the wreckage in sight. The plane was still afloat. He asked if the Canadians wanted his ship to attach a flotation collar to the plane and tow it back to Port Hardy.

Commander Pierstorff called Captain Waters on the radio.

"Captain Waters, it would be greatly appreciated if you would bring the plane to Port Hardy. Both pilots are convinced this was not a normal malfunction. Passengers included six prominent Kitasoo of international importance working hard to save the planet from climate change and pollution. Wild Bill was also on the plane when it ditched. We expect the TSB to go over that plane in great detail. We need to discover what caused the crash. Access to the plane's black box (flight recorder) would be a big help."

"Understood Commander. It should take my divers about an hour to attach a flotation collar. Once secured we will tow the plane to you. It will be about three hours before we arrive," said Captain Waters.

Once the plane was taken to Port Hardy, the USS Independence resumed her voyage to Alaska. Wild Bill Mendenhall and Commander Pierstorff both thanked Captain Steve Waters for his assistance.

The next day, two TSB investigators arrived in Port Hardy from Calgary. Inspectors downloaded and reviewed information from the plane's flight recorder. TSB officials inspected the engine and fuel tanks of the Pacifica plane. Maintenance records were forwarded from Anchorage, via internet, to Port Hardy.

Later that same day, TSB inspectors called a meeting with both pilots and Commander Pierstorff. Wild Bill was allowed to join the meeting.

"We know what caused the crash," said the senior TSB investigator.

"It was sabotage," said the lead investigator. "Sugar was in both fuel tanks. Enough sugar got by fuel filters and fuel pumps to affect the plane's performance. Sugar caused the pistons to seize. It was a dramatic and catastrophic engine failure. It is an inexact way to down a plane. Given enough time in the air, sugar can and will bring cause a plane to crash."

Commander Pierstorff placed a call to the RCMP. She asked for an official investigation, as attempted murder is a serious crime. She also called the United States Federal Bureau of Investigation (FBI) office in Anchorage and relayed the findings of sabotage. The RCMP and FBI promised to begin investigations immediately.

Wild Bill contacted Jim DeFord via the ship's radio and told him of the findings. DeFord agreed to stay in Klemtu until the RCMP and Tribal police could increase security for the Project HOPE directors.

It seemed certain that an individual or group, wanted to stop Project HOPE from succeeding. The list of potential suspects was exhaustive. The Kitasoo directors would have to be carefully guarded, until the criminals were apprehended.

KNOLHVAL AND SITKA

A rgonaut and Knolhval were swimming near Hanson Island when Knolhval turned to his son. "Son, do you read everyone's mind all the time or are you selective in your telepathy?" asked Knolhval.

"There is so much information and telepathic background noises that I only listen when I am called or when I need to respond to danger. It is hard to keep track of so many thoughts at one time. I have learned to block out most thoughts that surround me," said the Inua to his father.

"May I ask you a question?" asked Knolhval.

"Of course, father," said Argonaut.

"Why did you call me back to the pod. I have been gone for many seasons and I abandoned you," Knolhval said.

"Raven asked me about our family. He had a right to know history of his ancestors. The more I thought about our past, the more I realized how hard it must have been for you to lose a daughter and your mate. I missed having you in my life. I felt an emptiness that I could not fill. As my Inua powers grew, I could feel your presence, far away in the cold and darkness. I wanted you by my side so you could know me, Raven, Angel, and your great-grandson, Jason," Argonaut told his father.

"Are you happy I returned when you called?" asked Knolhval.

"I am very pleased that you are back in our sanctuary with your pod. We are family. Now we are together. I never want to be separated from you again, as long as we live," Argonaut told his father.

"I have another question to ask. Why doesn't Sitka have a mate? She is smart, strong, brave, and a wonderful matriarch. It seems to me any male would be happy to have her as his partner," said Knolhval.

"I am not sure. Ever since Spirit died, she has been busy taking care of our pod. She has never spoken of being lonely. Have you asked her about this?" Argonaut said to his father.

Knolhval said, "I have known Sitka since long before your birth. I had a wonderful mate in your mother. When she died, I thought I would always be alone. Now I realize I want to be happy, with a partner in my life."

"I think you should talk to her and see if she is interested in being your mate. You have been friends for many years. You do a wonderful job helping with the calves. You are brave. You proved this when facing the sick orca," Argonaut told his father.

"Thank you, son. I will ask if she is interested in joining me as my partner. I have much respect for her. I would be honored if she agreed to become my mate," Knolhval said.

The next day, Knolhval asked Sitka if he might swim with her and ask her a question

"Of course, old friend. Ask me whatever you wish. We have known each other all our lives. You are part of our pod," Sitka said.

"I would like you to become my partner. I have been alone too long. I have grieved many years for my first mate. It is time to find happiness with another female. You are the most wonderful humpback I know. Will you join me as my partner?' he asked.

Sitka stopped swimming and turned to face Knolhval. She swam right to his face. She touched noses with him. She was pleased.

"I do not know what took you so long. I have been waiting for you to ask me to join you since you returned," Sitka said.

Knolhval was so happy he breached again and again. He sang the most beautiful love song any humpback had ever heard.

Sitka gathered the pod and told them of her joining with Knolhval. The entire pod congratulated both Sitka and Knolhval. It was a good day in Johnstone Strait.

NEW STORIES FOR THE MEMORY KEEPER

Sitka and Argonaut swam near the pod late one evening. They were on night watch, keeping the pod safe.

Argonaut asked Sika if she had more stories for him to learn.

Sitka laughed and said, "There are always many more stories for you to learn."

"Will you tell me of the beginning of our kind?" asked Argonaut.

Sitka said, "Legends say, in the beginning, the world was only water and land. A great raven flew from the sky with seeds. Fish, trees, animals, and humans all appeared wherever the raven dropped his seeds. He flew over the entire world. Some seeds grew whales. Some grew orcas. Many different types of trees sprang from the seeds. All living things began with this ancient raven, as he dropped his seeds."

"Do you know the name of the raven?" Argonaut asked his matriarch.

"His name was Hrafn. He was first among the Inua. He is said to have lived for almost all time. His magic saved many people. Our human friends know the power of the raven," Sitka said.

Argonaut was stunned. He was at a loss for words. He stopped and stared at Sitka.

"What is it?" Sitka asked her Inua friend.

"I met Hrafn this season. He appeared to me and we talked. He told me he was an ancient Inua. He never said he was the first Inua. He said I was a great Inua. His time was over. I watched as he flew into the night sky. He became a new bright star, in the darkness above. I did not know the story of how he dropped seeds that started all life. Do you know where he got these seeds?" Argonaut asked.

Sitka told Argonaut, "Another part of the story is that a great spirit lives in the sky. She gave seeds to Hrafn. The great spirit was here before time began. She will last forever. She put the stars in the sky. She made both the sun and moon. She sees all. She is always with us. Those who know this legend call her, Torngasak," Sitka told Argonaut.

Sitka told Argonaut stories of many different spirits that she had learned in her training as a memory keeper. She told him of Aukaneck. This spirit is said to live in the sea and create waves by his movements. Aumanil is a spirit that lives on land and controls the movements of all whales. Tekkeitsertok is a great spirit of the earth and owns all the deer that humans and other creatures eat.

Argonaut asked his matriarch why there are many different types of whales and other creatures. Sitka shook her said and told Argonaut; she did not know.

"I think many creatures feed on other creatures. Orcas eat sea lions. Sea lions eat fish. Big fish eat smaller fish. We eat small fish. There is a master plan created by Torngasak. We are part of her plan. I am matriarch to our pod. You are Inua and help save many creatures. We each have a place in the world. As an Inua, you can see into the future. You know part of the plan before it happens. No one but an Inua knows what will happen tomorrow," said Sitka.

"It is sometimes good to see the future. I knew the orcas were going to attack our pod. I knew Angel was in peril. Sometimes I wish I were not Inua. I feel responsible for every whale in our pod. It is a burden to me. I am glad to be useful. Sometimes I do not want to see and hear so much," Argonaut said.

Sitka smiled. She knew how heavy the burden Argonaut carried. As matriarch, she also worried about her pod. She had many responsibilities.

Argonaut saw Angel swimming in the distance. He left Sitka to join his mate. It was a lovely summer day in the Johnstone Strait. Argonaut cleared his mind. As he swam to Angel she turned and rubbed noses with him.

"How are you, my mate?" she asked.

Argonaut answered, "I am always better when I am near you."

SABOTEURS DISCOVERED

Agents of the FBI and Alaska State Safety Department reviewed all surveillance footage from cameras observing the Pacifica private airfield in Anchorage. Surveillance video showed a single man approach the Piper Propjet that crashed carrying Kitasoo directors of Project HOPE and Wild Bill Mendenhall.

At 2:09 A.M. the morning of the crash, an unidentified individual did what appeared to be a safety check of the plane. Using freeze-frame technology and greatly enhanced images, agents discovered the sabotage.

The suspect had dropped a substance into both wing tanks of the Pacifica plane. He left the airfield at 2:41 A.M. Visitor logs showed no record of any authorized personnel entering restricted airfield property between midnight and 6 A.M. All maintenance technicians were interviewed. Their alibis had been verified.

Based on the height of the airplane, it was estimated the saboteur was approximately six-feet tall. There were no clear full-face pictures of the saboteur. There were several side-view images. Identification experts were able to run facial-recognition software on images captured by surveillance camera video footage.

A match of the face was found in the FBI criminal database. A man named Kevin Moody had been in prison three times. Moody was previously convicted of armed robbery, theft of an airplane, and assault with a deadly weapon. He was currently on parole. He lived in Soldotna, Alaska.

An FBI SWAT team arrested Moody, without incident, at his home early the next day. As was his right, the accused refused to answer questions until his attorney arrived. A public defender was appointed to represent Moody.

FBI Special Agent in Charge, Michael Berryhill, entered the interrogation room.

"Moody, we have video footage of you sabotaging the plane. We have a credit card receipt from a gas station two miles from the Anchorage airport on the night of the sabotage. You charged ten pounds of sugar at the local grocery store the day before you damaged the plane. We found fingerprints matching yours on the gas tank covers of the Piper Propjet.

We charge you with nine counts of attempted murder and one count of tampering with a commercial airplane. With your record, these charges are certain to result in a life sentence, with no hope of parole. You will do hard time in the maximum-security federal prison at Fort Leavenworth, Kansas. Do you have anything to say?" Berryhill asked.

Moody's lawyer said he wanted to confer with his client before he made any statements.

Berryhill left the room. A few minutes later the lawyer called him back to the interview room.

Moody said, "I am not admitting anything at this point. If, however, I did know something of a plane crash, including the brains behind it, could we make a deal?"

"You are a four-time loser. You have very little negotiating room. Any information you might be able to provide would need to be significant and verifiable, to reduce your sentence. The information would have to lead to an arrest and conviction. You would have to testify under oath at the individual's trial.

I could talk to the federal prosecutor. We might be able to shorten your prison stay. It is possible you could serve your sentence in a prison closer to your family in Alaska. I need some idea of what you know, before I talk to the prosecutor," Berryhill said.

"I may know who wanted the plane to crash. I might be able to give you his name, phone number, and address. Before I talk, I want a signed deal. Ten-year maximum sentence with time-off for good behavior. Five-years parole, after release. Can you make that happen?" asked Moody.

Berryhill looked at Moody with disgust.

"No promises. I will talk to the prosecutor and be back here within two hours," said the FBI agent.

After conferring with the federal prosecutor for the Ninth Circuit, Berryhill had a deal signed by the federal government. He returned to the jail and entered the interview room where Moody and his attorney were waiting.

"If I like what you have to say, if we find enough evidence to arrest, and convict the person you name, we have a deal," said Agent Berryhill.

Moody's attorney reviewed the agreement. He told Moody to disclose the facts of his involvement with the plane crash.

"I received a call from a burner phone two weeks ago. A voice said he had a job for me. Pay would be fifty-thousand dollars for a few minutes work. All I had to do was disable a plane. I would get half the money up front. Another twenty-five thousand once the job was done. We scheduled a meeting for midnight on June 1 in Kincaid Park. I was to come alone. I met the guy at the picnic tables near the back of the park. I went to the park the night before to set up four motion-activated night-vision cameras. I got sixteen shots of the guy. I followed him back to his car. I got a photo of his license plate. After I put sugar in the plane's wing tanks, I called the number he gave me. He gave me another twenty-five thousand dollars. We met at the same place. He again tripped the cameras. I got another twelve shots of him," Moody told the agent.

"Where are these pictures?" Berryhill asked.

"They are buried in an ammo can in my backyard. Ten paces west of the back door of my place. Buried next to the only spruce tree in my yard. They are stored on a USB drive wrapped in a plastic bag," said Moody.

"Do you have the name of the person behind the sabotage?" asked Berryhill.

"He called himself John Smith. My guess, that is not his real name," Moody replied.

"How did he find you?" Berryhill asked.

A cellmate from my last stint in prison gave him my name. The guy who got me the job is Jack Turner. He works as a bouncer at a dive on Fifth Street. He knows who hired me," Moody told the agent.

"We will get the photos, pick up your friend, trace the auto tag, and see if we can arrest the guy who paid you. You will be a guest of the federal government until we get our man," Berryhill said as he turned to leave the interrogation room.

"Hey, Berryhill. I had no idea there would be kids on that plane. I have grown kids of my own. I would never hurt kids," said Moody.

"If those people had died you would have gotten the maximum penalty under law. I would have buried you under the prison" said Berryhill as he turned and left.

Three days later they arrested Jake Trapper at his home in Juneau, Alaska. He was a black ops contractor for a group called Oil Price Support Confederation (OPSC). This large oil consulting group had contracts with all oil producing companies operating outside of North America. The FBI arrested the group's president, vice president, and chief financial officer. Under intense interrogation, the three confessed to attempting to stop Project HOPE. The FBI was able to trace the funds from OPSC to Moody. It was an open and shut case. The world oil consumers were starting to demand less oil and prices were falling. If OPSC couldn't stop falling petroleum product demand, it stood to lose millions of dollars in consulting fees.

All three men involved in the attempted murder plot were charged with first degree felonies. They are awaiting trial in Anchorage.

BIGGSY AND HER CALF NEED HELP

The excitement of the last few weeks had died down. The Kitasoo tribe received help from the Tribal Police, RCMP, Wild Bill Mendenhall and Captain Jim DeFord in providing round the clock protection for Project HOPE directors. Sabotage of the Pacifica plane carrying the directors made it clear, lives of the young Kitasoo were at risk. The HOPE efforts were making a difference. Some corporations and investors were losing vast sums of money because of Project HOPE. Success was being achieved in reducing fossil fuel demand.

The humpbacks were enjoying their summer. Fewer cruise ships were traversing the straits since the COVID-19 pandemic had reduced international travel. Bait fish were plentiful. Orcas and humpbacks lived in peace with each other.

Early one morning, Angel came to Argonaut with worry in her mind.

"Something is wrong with Biggsy and her calf. They seem ill. None of the other whales feel sick. Our daughter-in-law and grandson are not well," said Angel.

Argonaut went to the ailing whales. He asked them what was wrong. Neither whale could explain their illness. They felt weak, had no appetite, and were very tired.

Argonaut immediately called out to Jason. He explained the situation to his friend. Based on his knowledge and experience as a marine biologist, Jason had an idea what might be wrong. Since both a mother and her calf were involved, he was almost certain what was causing the illness. No other whales were exhibiting symptoms.

Jason called his friend Professor John Leibach at the University of Alaska, Southeast in Juneau. Leibach was chairman of the marine biology department and an expert on humpback whale anatomy.

Professor Leibach answered Jason's call.

"Hi, Jason. How are you?" Leibach said.

"I am fine, but we have two sick whales in our resident pod. I think I know what is wrong. I want to get a second opinion," Jason said.

"What's going on?" Leibach asked.

"A mother and her calf have the same symptoms. Lack of appetite, fatigue, and weakness. No other whales have the same signs. What do you think is wrong with them?" Jason asked.

"I am not a vet, but I think they have nematodes. The Latin name for the worm is Crassicaudosis. It is a common parasite found in the systems of mothers who pass it on to their young. If not caught, and treated in time, it can be fatal. It strikes many types of baleen whales, including humpbacks," Leibach said.

"That is exactly what I thought. I remember studying the illness when I took one of your classes as an undergraduate student. Is there a cure?" Jason asked.

"Yes. A drug of the Anthelmintic family is used with great success, if the illness is caught early enough. Basically, a large worm infects the anatomical system of the whales. If left untreated, there can be an infection of the whale's blood vessels. Eventually, there is loss of kidney function which can be fatal," Leibach explained.

"How can we get the drugs into the whales?" Jason asked.

"A vet will inject the drug into the whale. Within a few days recovery should occur. Usually a single dose of the medicine will kill the worm," Leibach said.

"Thank you, John. I will call Dr. Skip Foster who has helped with some of our sick whales in the past. I appreciate your confirming my diagnosis," Jason said.

Professor Leibach told Jason that Dr. Foster could take a blood sample from the whales for verification. However, he was almost positive that a nematode was the cause of the symptoms.

"How are you going to get a whale to stay still for a shot and a blood sample?" Leibach asked.

Jason said, "I have been swimming with this pod for many years. They know me by sight. They trust me."

"It is hard to imagine a sixty-thousand-pound whale sitting still for an injection and a blood sample. I would like to see that. Can you video the procedure and send me a copy?" said Leibach.

"I will try. Thank you, again," Jason said.

Jason's next call was to Dr. Skip Foster the preeminent marine veterinarian in western Canada.

"Skip, it's Jason Belliveau".

How are you?" Jason asked his friend.

"Hi, Jason. I am fine. How can I help?" said Dr. Foster.

We have two sick humpbacks near Telegraph Cove. He described the symptoms and his conversation with Professor Leibach.

"I think you both are correct. It is imperative we inject the drug into both whales before their kidneys are impaired. I have a full clinic today with several important procedures I must perform. Can you arrange for a pickup of the drug in Vancouver, transport it to Telegraph Cove, and inject the medicine? Also, I would like you to take blood samples from both whales if you can," said Dr. Foster.

"I will call Commander Pierstorff to ask if she has any helicopters flying north from Vancouver. If the Coast Guard can deliver the medicine, I can do the injections and take blood samples. I will send samples to you by plane from Port Hardy. Thanks, Skip," Jason said.

"I will have vials of the medicine at the Pacifica desk in Vancouver. The Coast Guard can pick up what you need there. Let me know if I can do anything else to help. I will analyze the blood samples and send the results to you as soon as possible," Dr. Foster told Jason.

Jason called Commander Pierstorff. He explained the need to get medicine from Vancouver to Port Hardy, as soon as possible, to help cure Biggsy and her calf.

"Captain Bruce Brient is scheduled to leave Vancouver in about two hours for a flight to Port Hardy. I will have him pick-up the medicine and drop it off in Telegraph Cove. He should be there in less than three hours," said Commander Pierstorff.

"Thank you, Commander. I will meet Captain Brient at the airport. I will let you know how things turn out. This is for two members of our special whale friend's family," Jason explained.

"Understood. Any whale friend of yours, is a whale friend of mine," said the Coast Guard officer.

Commander Pierstorff knew of the Inua Argonaut and his family.

In less than three hours, Captain Brient delivered the drugs to Jason. Argonaut was waiting outside the harbor.

He led Jason to his daughter-in-law and grandson. Jason did not need his scuba gear since both sick whales were lying on the surface. He put on his dry suit, mask, and fins.

Once Jason was in the water, Argonaut explained to the sick whales, they were going to feel a prick where the medicine would be injected. Each would feel a second small prick, when the blood sample was taken.

Jason proceeded to inject the whales. He took a blood sample from each.

"If we are right, they both should feel much better after one sunrise and sunset. Let me know tomorrow how they are. I am going to take the blood samples to Port Hardy so they can be flown to Dr. Foster in Vancouver. We need our diagnosis verified. If we are in time, both sick whales should make a full recovery," Jason told the Inua.

Argonaut reached out with his nose and touched Jason's outstretched hands.

"Again, you have saved my family. I am forever in your debt. Perhaps, someday I will be able to help you. Thank you," said Argonaut.

Jason left for Port Hardy aboard Sadie Princess.

As hoped, within twenty-four hours both mother and calf were feeling much better. Dr. Foster verified the diagnosis of a nematode invasion from the blood samples.

Angel went to her mate and thanked him for helping to save Biggsy and her young calf, Jason.

Argonaut told her that family is the most important thing in life.

CRISIS IN THE JOHNSTONE STRAIT

I t was dawn on August 13, when Argonaut sensed the speeding boats approaching from Vancouver. He reached out to read the minds of the passengers on the boat. Argonaut knew there was great danger to him from these strangers.

Argonaut called out to his pod. He told them to separate into three groups. Raven, T-Rex, and Sitka would each lead a group of humpbacks to different coves. Knolhval and Argonaut would remain near Telegraph Cove.

The whales separated into different groups as Argonaut requested. They swam as fast as they could to their designated hiding areas.

Argonaut's secret was in danger of being discovered. He had not been betrayed by Brigitte Fisher. His Inua power was potentially uncovered by a doctoral student at

Oregon State University. Bruce Rogers was writing his doctoral dissertation on humpback whale behavior. Rogers had spent several years combing records of humpback whale activity, in and around straits of Vancouver. He read stories of whales that fought orcas, great whites, and one that was kidnapped by pirates. The common element in each story, was mention of a whale named Argonaut. The A on his tail made Argonaut easily identifiable. Rogers continued his research by interviewing witnesses of the orca attack at Telegraph Cove. He spoke with ferry boat Captain Coral Denton about the accident with the sailboat and subsequent, alleged, rescue of survivors by orcas. Argonaut was seen in the area of the ferry accident. The whale that was kidnapped was known to be Argonaut's mate. Argonaut had been in the area when Angel was released.

Rogers was not certain what made Argonaut so unique and important, but he was determined to find out. If there was some humpback trait not previously identified that he could document, Rogers would gain immediate fame as a great scientist. His dissertation could become a best-selling book. Rogers was a brilliant scientist and determined researcher.

Argonaut knew boats were arriving to search for the humpback with an A on his tail. Argonaut asked his father to swim slowly and carefully towards the boats. Perhaps Knolhval could distract researchers by breaching near their boats.

Argonaut reached out to Jason. He asked his friend for help.

"There are people coming who know I am not a usual humpback whale. I have split the pod into separate groups. They are all hidden in coves and bays. Knolhval is trying to distract the boaters looking for me. Will you come and help me hide?" Argonaut asked.

"I will do better than that. I will ask Commander Pierstorff to send a Coast Guard cutter to intercept the boaters. Officers will do a random inspection of their boats. We should be able to delay them long enough for you to swim into the Pacific Ocean. I had an idea this might happen one day. I have a surprise for you. I will join you as soon as I can," Jason said.

Jason had long feared Argonaut would be uncovered as a special whale. In anticipation of this day, Jason had a disguise made for Argonaut. Using the many pictures, he had taken of Argonaut as a guide, Jason had ordered a tail cover made for the Inua. A 3D printer company in Seattle made a rubber tail cover that was almost entirely black with just a few white dots. There was no A on the tail cover. It was made to slip over Argonaut's tail. It was similar to a wet suit. Argonaut would be able to swim unimpeded. The famous Inua would be unrecognizable. Jason planned to give Argonaut a new nickname. He needed a new name after he donned his disguise. If they were lucky, Argonaut could live in peace.

Once Jason put the cover on Argonaut's tail there would be no way to identify him. Jason told the 3D printing company the cover was for a photography project Jason was working on.

Jason had the cover aboard Sadie Princess. Jason raced as fast as he could to join Argonaut, while observing safety regulations. Matt had joined Jason before they left Port Hardy. Putting the disguise on the Inua was going to be a two-person challenge. If you have ever worn a wet suit, you know how tight the rubber suit fits. The tail cover would be tighter than a wet suit.

"Argonaut, do you sense us?" Jason thought. He and Matt had just left the northern harbor of Vancouver and we entering the Pacific Ocean.

"I am close. Slow your boat. I will surface beside you shortly," Argonaut replied.

Matt spotted Argonaut. He told Jason to stop the boat. Argonaut rose slowly to the surface. He laid next to Sadie Princess.

"I have read your thoughts. I understand your plan. Anchor your boat and I will stay above the surface while you and Matt fit the cover over my tail. I have no wish to hide my identity. I am proud to be known as Argonaut the Inua. However, safety of the pod and sanctuary must be my first concern. Pride in my tail is not important if the disguise will help protect the pod," Argonaut thought to his two friends.

Matt and Jason put on their dry suits and scuba gear. They dove next to Argonaut. They began tugging on the tight-fitting tail cover over his large tail. After much grunting and groaning, the skintight cover finally slipped over Argonaut's tail. The A was no longer visible.

"Try diving a few times. Let's see how the cover holds up," Jason thought.

Argonaut dove, breached, and swam as fast and deep as he could. The cover worked perfectly. The Inua now had a permanent disguise that might keep his identity secret.

Argonaut thanked his friends. He started his journey back to his pod. Argonaut reached out to Angel and his pod. He told them what had happened. He explained to his family about his new disguise. He told them to stay in separate groups until he arrived.

Jason and Matt returned to the Johnstone Strait and met the Coast Guard cutter. It was finishing the inspection of the boats carrying the researchers.

Jason pulled Sadie Princess alongside the boat carrying the researcher, Bruce Rogers. Jason asked if they could help the searchers. Jason told the research crew that he and Matt have lived in the area almost their entire lives. They would be happy to help the scientists, if they could.

Rogers said, "I am doing my doctoral dissertation on humpbacks of British Columbia. I have pieced together stories of a whale with a large A on his tail that has been involved in numerous incidents that are quite unusual. If these rumors are true, the whale named Argonaut is remarkable. I want to find this whale and study it. Maybe I will even be able to take blood and tissue samples."

Jason said, "You are too late. Argonaut and his family were seen earlier this year swimming north towards

Alaska. No additional sightings have been reported. We would be happy to let you know if we see him in the sanctuary. Many other whales have also left this area. There are rumors of great white sharks swimming right outside the harbor entrance. It is possible, humpbacks left out of fear of great whites."

"Do you mind if I and my friends search the area? Maybe the whale has returned," Rogers said.

"Of course, please observe all go-slow signs. The Coast Guard is very strict about enforcing boat speed rules for safety of all marine life," Matt said.

Just then Argonaut, with his new disguise, swam by the researchers and his friends on Sadie Princess. He was not identified. He continued on his way to join Angel. After an all-day search, the disappointed scientists returned to Vancouver.

The pod regrouped that night. Argonaut explained in great detail how Jason and Matt had protected his Inua secret. Even if others discovered the rumors of Argonaut, he would no longer be identifiable in the Johnstone Strait because of his disguise.

Yet again, Jason had helped his large Inua friend.

Jason and Argonaut agreed that from today forward, Argonaut's new nickname was Michael. Jason explained to Argonaut that in human legends, a famous powerful Angel had been named Michael. Inua and Angels seem much the same to many people who know the stories of both creatures. Argonaut was pleased with his new nickname.

Jason explained what had happened to Captain Jim, Wild Bill, and Commander Pierstorff.

Orca Lab and MERS would from today forward identify the newly identified whale as Michael. The "new whale" was added to all the known whales of the area and would be identified by the almost all black tail with just a few white spots.

JASON IN TROUBLE

As October approached, cooler temperatures prevailed in Vancouver area waters. Tourists were still arriving in Telegraph Cove, to travel on the Leviathan. Humpbacks would soon be leaving for their winter home. Temperatures were still above normal. It appeared average daily temperatures would again set a record for the year across Canada.

As part of his volunteer Coast Guard Auxiliary duties, Jason was patrolling the northern end of Johnstone Strait. He was motoring aboard Sadie Princess, checking for speeding recreational boaters or boats approaching too close to wildlife. Several "SEE A BLOW, GO SLOW" signs had loosened from their mountings. Jason was repairing signs with new screws.

Suddenly, Jason felt a sharp pain in his lower right abdomen area. He had been suffering minor discomfort for several days. He thought he had just pulled a muscle.

He had ignored the pain, until now.

Crippling spasms caused Jason to fall to the deck of Sadie Princess. He could not move. He could barely breathe. He was not able to reach his radio. His phone was in his jacket in a forward storage locker. Jason thought it must be an attack of appendicitis. If his appendix burst, he could die.

Jason called out using his thoughts for Argonaut.

"Argonaut, I am very sick. I need help. I may die," he thought.

Jason hoped Argonaut could sense his pain and read his thoughts. He knew his Inua friend would help, if he could. Jason drifted in and out of consciousness.

Argonaut and his pod were near where Jason's boat had stopped. The Inua felt Jason's pain and heard his cry for help. He started swimming towards the boat. He asked Raven and Knolhval to join him.

The three whales reached Sadie Princess within minutes. Jason was immobile. Argonaut sensed the horrible pain that his friend was suffering.

"What can we do to help?" Argonaut asked his friend.

"Call out to Wild Bill, Matt, Captain Jim, and

Commander Pierstorff. I need to get to a doctor quickly, or I will die," Jason said.

Argonaut closed his eyes. He concentrated on calling out to four friends who knew his secret. He gave their location. He asked if they could help Jason.

Wild Bill was flying supplies in his helicopter from Port Hardy to Klemtu when he heard Argonaut's cry for help. He immediately banked the copter. He flew south towards Orca Lab. The whales and Jason were located about one mile south of Orca Lab.

Wild Bill called Commander Pierstorff.

"Peggy, did you get the call for help from Argonaut?" Mendenhall asked.

"I did. I called Nanaimo Hospital. They have a surgical team preparing for surgery as we speak. Can you get Jason there quickly?" she asked.

"I am flying solo. I have no way to get to the boat and help Jason aboard my copter without help," he said.

Argonaut heard the exchange. He spoke to both Pierstorff and Mendenhall.

"There are two other whales here with me. We can push the boat to shore. If the helicopter can land in an open area near Orca Lab, lab staff will be able to help get

Jason to the helicopter. How soon can you be here?" Argonaut asked Mendenhall.

"I can see Orca Lab now. I will be there in three minutes. How quickly can you get the boat to shore?" Mendenhall asked.

"I do not know how to tell time. We will push Jason's boat to shore as fast as we can. I can see Orca Lab so it should be soon," Argonaut said.

Commander Pierstorff called Orca Lab. Diane and Christie were on duty. The Coast Guard officer explained that Jason was very ill. Sadie Princess would be striking shore shortly. Wild Bill needed help transporting Jason from Sadie Princess to the helicopter. Diane and Christie promised to help carry Jason from the boat to the helicopter.

Argonaut, Raven, and Knolhval made one last push. The boat struck shore. The three whales quickly swam back into deeper waters before Orca Lab staff could see they had been pushing the boat.

Wild Bill landed the helicopter. Diane and Christie were bringing Jason to the landing area. Mendenhall helped the two lab workers get Jason strapped into the co-pilots seat. The copter immediately lifted off, for a short flight to Nanaimo Medical Center.

When the helicopter arrived at the hospital helipad, a team of physicians and nurses were waiting. Jason was lifted onto a stretcher. He was rushed to surgery. Dr. Marisa Mendenhall, Wild Bill's daughter, was the general surgeon on call. As soon as the anesthesiologist had Jason asleep, Dr. Mendenhall performed the appendectomy.

After surgery, Dr. Mendenhall spoke to her father, Wild Bill.

"That was close. Jason's appendix was ready to burst. If we had been a few minutes later, it might have been too late. Good job getting him here so quickly, Dad," she said.

"Thanks kid. Jason is a great friend. I knew he was in good hands with you doing the surgery. I will contact everyone in the area and update them. How long before he gets out of the hospital?" he asked.

"If there are no complications, we will release him in three days. He will need to take it easy for a few days. He should be back to normal within a week," Marisa told her father.

"I will be back in three days to fly him to Telegraph Cove. The Hawks will take care of Jason until he is ready to return to work. Love you," Mendenhall told his daughter.

"Love you too. See you in three days," Marisa said.

As Wild Bill was flying towards Klemtu with the supplies, he called Commander Pierstorff and told her Jason would make a full recovery.

"Thanks for all you did for our friend. Be safe and stay in touch" Commander Pierstorff said.

Argonaut had followed all the conversations. The Inua knew Jason would be healthy again. He reached out to thank Wild Bill and Commander Pierstorff for their help. Jason was still recovering from surgery, so Argonaut could not telepathically reach his best friend. Argonaut was relieved. He told the pod that Jason was safe and recovering.

A week later, Jason was back on Sadie Princess when Argonaut slowly rose beside the boat. He spoke to Jason who looked at his Inua friend with tears in his eyes.

"You saved me. Without you, Raven, and Knolhval I would have died on my boat. How can I ever repay you?" Jason asked.

"You helped saved Angel from the evil pirates. You cut Raven from the nets when he was drowning. You warned me of great whites entering waters of our home.

There is no debt to repay. We are friends. There is nothing I would not do for you," Argonaut thought.

"We make a great team. When will you be leaving for your winter home?" Jason asked.

"Soon. Sitka wants us to feed as much as we can before our journey. I will miss you," Argonaut said.

"I will miss you too. Life seems much less exciting when you are gone," Jason told Argonaut.

"Rest my friend. I will contact you before we leave," Argonaut said.

The Inua left to join his pod. Whales continued to rest and feed in preparation for the long journey to Hawaii. A few days later Argonaut told Jason they would be leaving at dawn the following morning from Telegraph Cove to swim across the Pacific. Jason said he would be at the harbor entrance, to wish the pod a safe trip.

At dawn, Captain Jim, Matt, and Mary were aboard Orcella 2. Jason was waiting nearby on Sadie Princess. Two familiar boats followed the pod as whales started swimming towards the northern harbor of Vancouver Island.

Argonaut had told orcas, dolphins, and great whites his pod was leaving for the winter. He wished them well.

He said his pod would return when the weather was warm.

Argonaut was surprised, which does not happen often, when several pods of orcas, including residents and transients, met Sitka's group.

"May we swim with you for a short distance? We have much respect for Argonaut. We want to honor him for all he has done for our kind," said the oldest orca.

Dolphins also asked to join orcas in swimming with whales for a short distance. They, too, wanted to honor the Inua who had done so much to help both humans and marine life of the sanctuary.

Just as the large group of whales, orcas, and dolphins left the harbor, followed by Jason and the Hawk family, great whites approached. The sharks bowed to Argonaut and asked if they could join the other wildlife swimming with Argonaut.

Argonaut explained to the Hawks, Jason, and his pod what was happening.

"It is an honor to be your friend and to have you swim with us. I will miss all of you. Stay safe. We will be back as soon as Sitka tells us it is time," Argonaut told the gathered group of marine life.

For a few miles, the huge group swam together. Slowly each species separated from the whales. They returned to their homes.

Argonaut thanked the Hawks and Jason for all their help and friendship. He promised to call out as soon as the pod was back in Vancouver waters.

"Goodbye for now, my friend. See you in the spring," Jason said.

Orcella 2 and Sadie Princess started the return journey to Telegraph Cove. Argonaut and his pod slowly swam west towards Hawaii. It had been an exciting year.

Dark visions appeared in Argonaut's thoughts. He knew his life was in great danger when he returned to Vancouver. For now, he would just enjoy being with his father, his mate, his son, and the entire Sitka pod.

THE END

Here is a brief sample of what is to come in the third book about Argonaut, Jason, and all the other creatures of the Vancouver Island straits.

DEATH OF AN INUA

Argonaut saw the boat approaching Little Rex at high speed. People on the boat were in violation of sanctuary rules. They were a danger to all marine wildlife in the area.

Argonaut called out using his powerful Inua mind. He told Little Rex to dive as quickly as he could to avoid oncoming danger. The young humpback was so focused on chasing a bait ball of food that he ignored the Inua.

Argonaut used his Inua powers to try and reach the people on the boat. They had been drinking alcohol, had headphones on listening to music, so Argonaut could not reach into their minds.

Argonaut started swimming as quickly as he could to save Little Rex. It was going to be close. Argonaut dove so he could breach to try and lift Little Rex away from the oncoming boat.

Little Rex turned and looked with fright as the speeding boat approached him. Suddenly he felt himself lifted out of the water as Argonaut rose from the depths. Argonaut took the young calf in his mouth and threw him to safety.

The thirty-foot speed boat struck Argonaut on his right side while he was still above the water's surface. The bow broke six of Argonaut's ribs and his right lung was punctured by several broken bones. The propeller of the boat cut him deeply.

The Inua was stunned. He was briefly knocked unconscious. T-Rex had seen Argonaut save his son. He swam to his friend who lay dying in Johnstone Strait. T-Rex called out to Sitka and the rest of the pod using whale vocalizations.

As the whales gathered around Argonaut, he slowly recovered consciousness. He was severely injured. He knew without help he might die. Argonaut told other mature humpbacks to push him towards Hanson Island.

While others were pushing him to shallow water, he reached out to Jason.

"I am hurt. I was hit by a boat and I may die. I have trouble breathing. I cannot feel one side of my body. I am not afraid of death, if this is my time. There is so much more I want to do before I go to the sacred ancient burial grounds. Can you help, please?" Argonaut said to Jason.

The whale who had saved Jason's life and so many others was in danger of dying.

PREVIEW: DEATH OF AN INUA

Made in the USA
Columbia, SC
26 July 2020